HERTA MÜLLER was born in Timis, Romania in 1953. A vocal member of the German minority, she was forced to leave the country in 1987, and moved to Berlin, where she still lives. This edition of *The Passport* was the first publication of Müller's work in English. She is the 2009 winner of the Nobel Prize for Literature.

MARTIN CHALMERS (1948–2014) was a translator and for many years an adviser to Serpent's Tail. It was on his recommendation that Serpent's Tail published Herta Müller and Elfriede Jelinek, both of whom went on to win the Nobel Prize for Literature.

PAUL BAILEY was a Literary Fellow at the Universities of Newcastle and Durham, and a recipient of the E.M. Forster Award. His books have received critical acclaim. *At the Jerusalem* won the Somerset Maugham Award and an Arts Council Writers' Award, *Peter Smart's Confessions* was shortlisted for the 1977 Booker Prize and *Gabriel's Lament* for the 1986 Booker Prize. His latest novel, *The Prince's Boy*, was published in 2014.

Praise for Herta Müller

"With the concentration of poetry and the frankness of prose, Müller depicts the language of the dispossessed" Jury of the Nobel Prize for Literature

"Appropriately on the side of underdogs from Ceauşescu's dystopia to Ukrainian labour camps... so opening the eyes of non-German readers to new worlds. And that, from *Beowulf* to Müller, is a noble as well as a Nobel function of literature" *The Times*

"Especially now, 20 years after the fall of the Berlin Wall, it's a beautiful signal that such high quality literature and this life experience are being honoured" Angela Merkel

"[Müller's] dark, closely observed and sometimes violent work often explores exile and the grim quotidian realities of life under Ceauşescu... Her sensibility is often bleak, but the detail in her fiction can whip it alive" *New York Times*

"Müller has an eye for the surreal detail of a police state and has made it into strong, muscular literature" *The Times*

Praise for *The Passport*

"Müller is courageous and has summoned her surrealist imagination to brilliant effect when exposing the horrors of totalitarianism... *The Passport*, which was published in Berlin in 1986, months before she fled Romania, is an almost allegorical elegy of village life dominated by the need to escape... Müller uses the quality of European folk tale to brilliant effect. Set in a German village in Romania where the people dream of a different life in the West, the story is true to any country in which fantasy is the only escape from oppression... Politics and truth-telling, the courage of the witness and the weight of the message often decides the Nobel Literature Prize; in Herta Müller all of these elements are present, yet so too is the artist as the lone voice beckoning, intent on telling a story, on shaping a word picture" Eileen Battersby, *Irish Times*

"Herta Müller's language is the purest poetry. Every sentence has the rhythm of poetry, indeed is a poem or a painting" *Nurnerger Nachrichten*

"Herta Müller portrays a community that is breaking up, a dying village whose German inhabitants all seek to emigrate. At the centre stands the miller Windisch waiting for his passport. Bribing the mayor with sacks of flour proved in vain – so, now, in a rage of helplessness, he has to allow his daughter to visit the militiaman and the priest, to search for passports and baptismal certificates in their beds. The dirty realities of a totalitarian state... a chilling, far-sighted and lyrical graveside speech for a sad village in a sad land" *Neue Zurcher Zeitung*

THE PASSPORT

HERTA MÜLLER

Translated by Martin Chalmers

Foreword by Paul Bailey

First published in Great Britain in this translation in 1989
by Serpent's Tail, an imprint of Profile Books Ltd
3 Holford Yard
Bevin Way
London
WC1X 9HD
www.serpentstail.com

First published as *Der Mensch ist ein grosser Fasan auf der Wels* in 1986
by Rotbuch Verlag, Berlin

1 3 5 7 9 10 8 6 4 2

Designed and typeset by sue@lambledesign.demon.co.uk
Printed and bound by CPI Group (UK) Ltd, Croydon CR0 4YY

A CIP record for this book can
be obtained from the British Library

ISBN 978 1 78125 527 8
eISBN 978 1 84765 249 2

Mixed Sources
Product group from well-managed
forests and other controlled sources
www.fsc.org Cert no. TT-COC-062227
© 1996 Forest Stewardship Council
FSC

FOREWORD
by Paul Bailey

I

The Passport is the shortest and bleakest of Herta Müller's short, bleak books. The people who function in its densely compressed scenes are each of them scarred in some way. They are, essentially, victims – of war; of what we now call ethnic cleansing; and of the uniquely crazy form of totalitarianism that marked the years when the regime led by Nicolae Ceauşescu was in power in Romania. They are known as Swabians and they belong to a German-speaking minority. The villagers are outcasts in the province of Banat which they have known since birth and in which those who are unable to escape, for any number of unhappy reasons, will die. This novel is about many things, but at the core of the narrative is the story of a miller named Windisch who is set on taking his wife and daughter to a city in west Germany – Munich, or Stuttgart, perhaps – where a better life awaits them. He needs a passport in order to leave the country, and to attain it he must bribe the mayor with sacks of flour. The militiaman and the priest, two other powerful pillars of the benighted community, require something else from him before the precious little book can become his guarantee of freedom. They remind the desperate man that he has an attractive daughter, Amalie, who has it within her means to expedite the process satisfactorily. He understands all too clearly what the men are demanding.

That's the plot, so to speak. A more conventional writer would have used it as a device to accommodate suspense of the page-turning variety, with a murder or two to excite the reader's interest. But Herta Müller's often elliptical prose works to a different purpose. She is determined to give voice to those who were rendered voiceless by the state. Romanians of Hungarian and German origin were made aware, in the aftermath of the Second World War and beyond, that they were less second-class citizens than unwanted visitors. The heady references to racial purity that informed Ceauşescu's vainglorious addresses to parliament only exacerbated the division between the pure and the impure. The "pure", it has to be recorded, had a miserable time when Nicolae and his truly ghastly consort Elena were proclaiming themselves the Father and Mother of the radiant nation, but the "impure" had it much, much worse.

If *The Passport* (the German title of which can be translated literally as "Man is a Large Pheasant in the World") often reads like a medieval morality or a dark fairy story resurrected by the Brothers Grimm, then that is again intentional on Müller's part. Her characters aren't involved in a recognizable bourgeois society, for all that a few of them have telephones and television sets. An owl hovering over the village is a harbinger of death, as it would have been in centuries past. The superstitions of a bygone age are afforded everyday significance. Women are whores or household drudges, or both, while the men earn the risible wages for their toil that were made even more risible under Communism. Nothing changes, because nothing is expected to change.

II

The Passport is a deeply political novel, but not overtly so. There is no "message", as such. Once, and only once, does the author make plain her loathing of the peculiar kind of Stalinesque communism that held sway in Romania during her adolescent years and beyond. Amalie is spouting the party line to her young charges in primary school, as a thousand other teachers were ordered to do in the 1970s and 80s:

> Amalie points at the map. "This is our Fatherland," she says. With her fingertip she searches for the black dots on the map. "These are the towns of our Father-land," says Amalie. "The towns are the rooms of this big house, our country. Our fathers and mothers live

in our houses. They are our parents. Every child has its parents. Just as the father in the house in which we live is our father, so Comrade Nicolae Ceauşescu is the father of our country. And just as the mother in the house in which we live is our mother, so Comrade Elena Ceauşescu is the mother of our country. Comrade Nicolae Ceauşescu is the father of all the children. And Comrade Elena Ceauşescu is the mother of all the children. All the children love Comrade Nicolae and Comrade Elena, because they are their parents."

Amen. Herta Müller is acknowledging here that her own satirical powers are as nothing when compared to the absurdities otherwise intelligent and responsible citizens were commanded, by law, to speak by rote. You couldn't make it up, as tabloid journalists are fond of observing. For the Romania that began to be history at Christmas 1989 was a made-up place, the lunatic creation of two deluded monsters and their craven, fawning followers. It was the distinguished Romanian essayist and novelist Norman Manea who pointed out in his important book *On Clowns* that it was Ceauşescu's rare achievement to present himself as a pillar of benevolent sanity in a country where the ungrateful were deemed mad. In fact, as I can attest, the writers and teachers and actors I met in the months before the revolution all used the word about themselves. "He makes us all think we are mad," they said, with varying degrees of irony, "because that's the way he wants it."

The great poet George Bacovia defined Romania as a "sad country, full of humour". Herta Müller gives literary expression to that sadness, verging on hopelessness, in *The Passport*. The humour she records is of the last-ditch kind – the humour that looks horror in the face without turning away from it.

The white appears in the eyelid fissure between East and West. The pupil is not to be seen.

INGEBORG BACHMANN

THE POT HOLE

Around the war memorial are roses. They form a thicket.
So overgrown that they suffocate the grass. Their
blooms are white, rolled tight like paper. They rustle.
Dawn is breaking. Soon it will be day.

Every morning, as he cycles alone along the road to the
mill, Windisch counts the day. In front of the war memorial
he counts the years. By the first poplar tree beyond it, where
he always hits the same pot hole, he counts the days. And
in the evening, when Windisch locks up the mill, he counts
the years and the days once again.

He can see the small white roses, the war memorial and
the poplar tree from far away. And when it is foggy, the
white of the roses and the white of the stone is close in
front of him as he rides. Windisch rides on. Windisch's face
is damp, and he rides till he's there. Twice the thorns on
the rose thicket were bare and the weeds underneath were
rusty. Twice the poplar was so bare that its wood almost
split. Twice there was snow on the paths.

Windisch counts two years by the war memorial and
two hundred and twenty-one days in the pot hole by the
poplar.

Every day when Windisch is jolted by the pot hole,

he thinks, "The end is here." Since Windisch made the decision to emigrate, he sees the end everywhere in the village. And time standing still for those who want to stay. And Windisch sees that the night watchman will stay beyond the end.

And after Windisch has counted two hundred and twenty-one days and the pot hole has jolted him, he gets off for the first time. He leans the bicycle against the poplar tree. His steps are loud. Wild pigeons flutter out of the churchyard. They are as grey as the light. Only the noise makes them different.

Windisch crosses himself. The door latch is wet. It sticks to Windisch's hand. The church door is locked. Saint Anthony is on the other side of the wall. He is carrying a white lily and a brown book. He is locked in.

Windisch shivers. He looks down the street. Where it ends, the grass beats into the village. A man is walking at the end of the street. The man is a black thread walking into the field. The waves of grass lift him above the ground.

THE EARTH FROG

The mill is silent. The walls are silent and the roof is silent. And the wheels are silent. Windisch has pressed the switch and put out the light. Between the wheels it is night. The dark air has swallowed the flour dust, the flies, the sacks.

The night watchman is sitting on the mill bench. He's sleeping. His mouth is open. The eyes of his dog gleam under the bench.

Windisch carries the sack with his hands and with his knees. He leans it against the wall of the mill. The dog looks and yawns. Its white teeth set wide.

The key turns in the keyhole of the mill door. The lock clicks between Windisch's fingers. Windisch counts. Windisch feels his temples beating and thinks, "My head is a clock." He puts the key in his pocket. The dog barks. "I'll wind it up, till the spring snaps," says Windisch out loud.

The night watchman presses his hat down onto his forehead. He opens his eyes and yawns. "Soldier on guard duty," he says.

Windisch walks over to the mill pond. At the edge is a stack of straw. A dark blot on the reflection in the pond. The blot goes down into the depths like a crater. Windisch pulls his bicycle out of the straw.

"There's a rat in the straw," says the night watchman. Windisch picks the blades of straw from the saddle. He throws them into the water. "I saw it," he says, "it threw itself into the water." The blades float like hair. They turn in small eddies. The dark crater floats. Windisch looks at his moving reflection.

The night watchman kicks the dog in the stomach. The

dog yelps. Windisch looks into the crater and hears the yelping under the water. "The nights are long," says the night watchman. Windisch takes a step backwards. Away from the edge. He sees the unchanging picture of the stack of straw, facing away from the edge. It is still. It has nothing to do with the crater. It is paler than the night.

The newspaper rustles. The night watchman says, "My stomach is empty." He takes out some bread and bacon. The knife flashes in his hand. He chews. He scratches his wrist with the blade of the knife.

Windisch wheels the bicycle along. He looks at the moon. Still chewing, the night watchman quietly says, "A man is nothing but a pheasant in the world." Windisch lifts the sack and lays it on the bicycle. "A man is strong," he says, "stronger than the beasts."

A corner of the newspaper is flying loose. The wind tugs like a hand. The night watchman lays the knife on the bench. "I slept a little," he says. Windisch is bent over his bicycle. He raises his head.

"And I woke you," he says.

"Not you," says the night watchman, "my wife woke me." He brushes the breadcrumbs from his jacket. "I knew," he says, "that I wouldn't be able to sleep. The moon is large. I dreamt of the dry frog. I was dead tired. And I couldn't get to sleep. The earth frog was lying in bed. I was talking to my wife. The earth frog looked with my wife's eyes. It had my wife's plait. It had her nightshirt on, which had ridden up to the stomach. I said: 'Cover yourself, your thighs are flabby.' I said it to my wife. The earth frog pulled the nightshirt over its thighs. I sat down on the chair beside the bed. The earth frog smiled with my wife's mouth. 'The chair is creaking,' it said. The chair hadn't creaked. The earth frog had laid my wife's plait across its shoulder. It was as long as the nightshirt. I said: 'Your hair has grown.' The earth frog raised its head and shouted: 'You're drunk, you're going to fall off the chair.'"

The moon has a red patch of cloud. Windisch leans against the wall of the mill. "Men are stupid," says the night watchman, "and always ready to forgive." The dog eats a bacon rind. "I forgave her over the baker. I forgave her for what happened in town." He strokes the blade of the knife with his finger tip. "The whole village laughed at me." Windisch sighs. "I couldn't look her in the eye anymore," says the night watchman. "Only one thing I didn't forgive her – that she died so quickly, as if she'd had no one."

"God knows," says Windisch, "what they're for, women."

The night watchman shrugs his shoulders: "Not for us," he says. "Not for me, not for you. I don't know who they're for." The night watchman strokes the dog.

"And our daughters," says Windisch. "God knows, they become women too."

There's a shadow on the bicycle, and a shadow on the grass. "My daughter," says Windisch, weighing the sentence in his head, "my Amalie is no longer a virgin either." The night watchman looks at the red patch of cloud. "My daughter has calves like melons," says Windisch. "As you said, I can't look her in the eye any more. There's a shadow in her eyes." The dog turns its head.

"Eyes lie," says the night watchman, "but calves don't." He places his feet apart. "Watch how your daughter walks," he says. "If the toes of her shoes point outwards when she puts her feet on the ground, then it's happened."

The night watchman turns his hat in his hand. The dog lies and watches. Windisch is silent. "Dew is falling. The flour will get damp," says the night watchman, "the mayor will be annoyed."

A bird is flying over the pond. Slow and straight, as if drawn along on a string. Close to the water. As if it were ground. Windisch follows it with his eyes. "Like a cat," he says.

"An owl," says the night watchman. He puts his hand to his mouth. "The light at Widow Kroner's has been burning for three nights." Windisch pushes his bicycle.

"She can't die," he says, "the owl hasn't settled on any roof yet."

Windisch walks through the grass and looks at the moon. "I'm telling you, Windisch," calls the night watchman, "women deceive."

THE NEEDLE

The light is still burning in the joiner's house. Windisch stops. The window pane shines. It reflects the street. It reflects the trees. The picture passes through the lace curtain. Through its falling posies of flowers into the room. A coffin lid leans against the wall beside the tiled stove. It's waiting for the death of Widow Kroner. Her name is written on the lid. The room seems empty despite the furniture, because it's so bright.

The joiner is sitting on a chair with his back to the table. His wife is standing in front of him. She is wearing a striped nightshirt. She's holding a needle in her hand. A grey thread hangs from the needle. The joiner is holding out his forefinger to his wife. The woman is picking a splinter of wood out of his flesh with the point of the needle. The forefinger bleeds. The joiner pulls his finger back. The woman lets the needle fall. She lowers her eyes and laughs. The joiner grasps under her nightshirt with his hand. The nightshirt rides up. The stripes wriggle. The joiner grasps at his wife's breasts with his bleeding finger. Her breasts are large. They tremble. The grey thread hangs on the chair leg. The needle swings, its point facing downwards.

The bed is beside the coffin lid. The pillow is made of damask. Spots are scattered across it, large ones and small ones. The sheet is white and the bedspread is white.

The owl flies past the window. One beat of its wings carries it across the pane. It twitches in flight. The light falls at an angle, and the owl becomes two.

Bent over, the woman walks up and down in front of the table. The joiner grabs her between the legs. The woman sees the needle hanging. She reaches for it. The thread sways. The woman lets her hand slide down her body. She closes her eyes. She opens her mouth. The joiner pulls her into bed by the wrist. He throws his trousers onto the chair. His underpants are stuffed into the trouser legs like a white rag. The woman opens her thighs and bends her knees. Her stomach is made of dough. Her legs are a white window frame on the sheet.

A picture in a black frame hangs over the bed. The headscarf of the joiner's mother lies against the rim of her husband's hat. The glass has a spot. The spot is on her chin. She smiles out of the picture. Close to death, she smiles. In less than a year. She smiles through the wall into the room.

The wheel of the well is turning, because the moon is large and is drinking the water. Because the wind is in its spokes. The sack is damp. It hangs over the rear wheel like a sleeping man. "The sack hangs behind me like a dead man," thinks Windisch.

Windisch feels his stiff, obstinate member against his thigh.

"The joiner's mother," thinks Windisch, "has cooled down."

THE WHITE DAHLIA

In the heat of August, the joiner's mother had lowered a big melon into the well in a pail. The well made waves around the pail. Water gurgled around the green skin. The water cooled the melon.

The joiner's mother had gone into the garden with the big knife. The garden path was a furrow. The lettuce had shot up. Their leaves were stuck together by the white milk that forms in the stems. The joiner's mother had carried the knife down the furrow. Where the fence begins and the garden ends, a white dahlia bloomed. The dahlia reached up to her shoulder. The joiner's mother smelt the dahlia. She smelt at the white leaves for a long time. She breathed in the dahlia. She rubbed her forehead and looked into the yard.

The joiner's mother cut the white dahlia with the big knife.

"The melon was just a pretext," said the joiner after the funeral. "The dahlia was her misfortune." And the joiner's neighbour said, "The dahlia was a vision."

"Because it was so dry that summer," said the joiner's wife, "all the dahlia's leaves were white and closed up. Its flower was larger than any dahlia can be. And because there was no wind that summer, it didn't drop off. The dahlia had long breathed its last, yet it couldn't wither."

"You can't stand it," said the joiner, "no one can stand it."

No one knows what the joiner's mother did with the dahlia she had cut off. She didn't bring the dahlia into the house. She didn't put it in the room. She didn't leave it lying in the garden either.

"She came out of the garden. She had the big knife in her hand," said the joiner. "There was something of the dahlia in her eyes. The whites of her eyes were dry."

"It may be," said the joiner, "that she was waiting for the melon and plucked the dahlia to pieces. Plucked it apart with her hands. Not a single petal lay scattered on the ground. As though the garden were a room."

"I believe," said the joiner, "that she scraped a hole in the ground with the big knife. She buried the dahlia."

The joiner's mother had pulled the pail out of the well late in the afternoon. She carried the melon to the kitchen table. She stabbed into its green skin with the point of the knife. She turned her arm and the big knife in a circle and cut the melon through the middle. The melon cracked. It was a death rattle. In the well, on the kitchen table, until its two halves were split apart, the melon had still been alive.

The joiner's mother had opened her eyes wide. Because her eyes were as dry as the dahlia, they did not grow large. The juice dripped from the blade of the knife. Her eyes were small and full of hate as she looked at the red flesh. The black seeds lay above one another like the teeth of a comb.

The joiner's mother had not cut the melon into slices. She placed the two halves in front of her. She dug the red flesh out with the point of the knife. "She had the greediest eyes I've ever seen," said the joiner.

The red water had dripped over the kitchen table. Dripped from the corners of her mouth. Dripped down from her elbows. The floor was sticky from the red water of the melon.

"My mother's teeth had never been so white and cold," said the joiner. "She ate and said: 'Don't look at me like that, don't look at my mouth.' She was spitting the black seeds onto the table."

"I looked away. I didn't leave the kitchen. I was frightened of the melon," said the joiner. "I looked out of the window into the street. Someone I didn't know was walking past. He was walking quickly and talking to himself. I heard my mother digging with the knife. Heard her chewing. And swallowing. 'Mother,' I said without looking at her, 'stop eating.'"

The joiner's mother had raised her hand. "She screamed, and I looked at her, because she'd screamed so loudly," said the joiner. "She threatened me with the knife. 'This is no summer, and you're no man,' she screamed. 'My temples are throbbing. My bowels are burning. This summer is throwing out the fire of many years. Only the melon cools me down.'"

THE SEWING MACHINE

The pebbles are uneven and small. The owl cries behind the trees. It's looking for a roof. The houses stand white and streaked with lime.

Windisch feels the obstinate member below his navel. The wind knocks on the wood. It's sewing. The wind is sewing a sack in the earth.

Windisch hears his wife's voice. She says: "Monster." Every night when Windisch turns his breath towards her in bed, she says: "Monster." For two years she has had no uterus in her stomach. "The doctor told me not to," she says, "I'm not going to let my insides be messed about just to please you."

When she says it, Windisch feels a cold anger between her face and his. She grasps Windisch by the shoulder. Sometimes it takes a while before she finds his shoulder. When she has found Windisch's shoulder she says in the darkness close to Windisch's ear, "You could be a grandfather by now. Our time has passed."

The previous summer, Windisch had been on his way home with two sacks of flour.

Windisch had knocked at a window. The mayor shone his torch through the curtain. "Why do you still knock?" said the mayor. "Put the flour in the yard. The gate is open." His voice was asleep. That night, there was a thunderstorm.

A flash of lightning struck the grass in front of the window. The mayor switched off his torch. His voice woke up and spoke more loudly. "Another five deliveries, Windisch," said the mayor, "then the money at New Year. And at Easter you'll have your passport." There was a roll of thunder and the mayor looked up to the window. "Put the flour underneath the roof," he said, "it's going to rain."

"Twelve deliveries since then, and ten thousand lei, and Easter is long past," thinks Windisch. It's a long time since he knocked on the window. He opens the gate. Windisch presses the sack to his stomach and puts it in the yard. Even when it's not raining, Windisch puts the sack underneath the roof.

His bicycle is light. Windisch holds it close to him, as he wheels it along. When the bicycle is going through the grass, Windisch can't hear his footsteps.

That night, all the windows had been dark. Windisch had stood in the long hallway. A flash of lightning tore open the earth. A roll of thunder pressed the house down into the crevice. Windisch's wife didn't hear the key turning in the lock.

Windisch had stood in the hall. The thunder was so far above the village, beyond the gardens, that there was a cold stillness in the night. The pupils in his eyes were cold. Windisch had the feeling that the night was going to shatter, that all at once it would be dazzlingly bright above the village. Windisch stood in the hall and knew that if he had not gone into the house, he would have seen, across all the gardens, the narrow end of all things and his own end everywhere.

Behind the door Windisch heard the stubborn, regular moaning of his wife. Like a sewing machine.

Windisch flung the door open. He switched on the light. His wife's legs, raised on the sheet, were like open window sashes. They twitched in the light. Windisch's wife opened her eyes wide. Her gaze was not dazzled by the light. It was merely fixed.

Windisch bent down. He unlaced his shoes. He looked beneath his arm at his wife's thighs. He saw her pulling a slimy finger out of the hair. She didn't know where to put the hand with the finger. She laid it on her naked stomach.

Windisch looked down at his shoes and said: "So that's how it is with your bladder, my lady." Windisch's wife put the hand with that finger to her face. She pushed her legs down to the foot of the bed. She pressed them closer and closer together, until Windisch could see only a single leg and the two soles of her feet.

Windisch's wife turned her face to the wall and wept loudly. She wept for a long time with the voice of her younger years. She wept briefly and softly with the voice of her own age. She whimpered three times with the voice of another woman. Then she was silent.

Windisch switched off the light. He climbed into the

warm bed. He felt her slime, as if she had emptied her stomach into the bed.

Windisch heard sleep pressing her down far below this slime. Only her breath hummed. He was tired and empty. And far from all things. The sound of her breath seemed to be at the end of all things, at his own end.

That night her sleep was so distant, that no dream could find her.

BLACK SPOTS

The skinner's windows are behind the apple tree. They are brightly lit. "He's got his passport," thinks Windisch. The windows glare and the glass is naked. The skinner has sold everything. The rooms are empty. "They've sold the curtains," says Windisch to himself.

The skinner is leaning against the tiled stove. There are white plates on the floor. Cutlery is lying on the window-sill. The skinner's black coat is hanging on the door handle. The skinner's wife bends over the large suitcases as she passes. Windisch can see her hands. They throw shadows against the empty walls of the room. They grow long and bend. Her arms are rippled like branches over water. The skinner is counting his money. He lays the bundles of notes in the pipes of the tiled stove.

The cupboard is a white rectangle, the beds are white frames. The walls in between are black patches. The floor slopes. The floor rises. It rises high against the wall. And stops at the door. The skinner is counting the second bundle of money. The floor will cover him. The skinner's wife blows the dust from the grey fur cap. The floor will lift her to the ceiling. By the tiled stove, the clock has struck a long white patch against the wall. Windisch closes his eyes. "Time is at an end," he thinks. He hears the white patch of the clock on the wall ticking and sees a clock-face of black spots. Time has no clock hand. Only the black spots are turning. They crowd together. They push themselves out of the white patch. Fall along the wall. They are the floor. The black spots are the floor in the other room.

Rudi is kneeling on the floor in the empty room. Before him, coloured glass lies in long rows. In circles. Beside Rudi is the empty suitcase. A picture is hanging on the wall. It isn't a picture. The frame is made of green glass. Inside the frame is frosted glass with red waves.

The owl flies over the gardens. Its cry is high. Its flight is deep. Its flight is full of night. "A cat," thinks Windisch, "a cat that flies."

Rudi holds a spoon of blue glass to his eye. The white of his eye grows large. His pupil is a wet, glistening sphere in the spoon. The floor washes colours to the edge of the room. The time from the other room beats waves. The black spots float along. The light bulb flickers. The light is torn. The two windows swim into one another. The two floors push the walls in front of them. Windisch holds his head in his hand. His pulse is beating in his head. His temple beats in his wrist. The floors lift themselves. They come closer, touch. They sink down into the crack. They will be heavy, and the earth will break. The glass will glow, will become a trembling abscess in the suitcase.

Windisch opens his mouth. He feels them growing in his face, the black spots.

THE BOX

Rudi is an engineer He worked in a glass factory for three years. The glass factory is in the mountains.

During those three years the skinner only visited his son once. "I'm going to visit Rudi in the mountains for a week," the skinner had said to Windisch.

The skinner came back after three days. He had ruddy cheeks from the mountain air and tired eyes from lack of sleep. "I couldn't sleep there," said the skinner. "I didn't sleep a wink. I could feel the mountains in my head' at night."

"Everywhere you look," explained the skinner, "there are mountains. On the way to the mountains are tunnels. They are black as night. The train goes through the

tunnels. The whole mountain rattles in the train. You get
a buzzing in your ears and throbbing in your head. First
pitch black night, then broad daylight," said the skinner,
"and constantly alternating. It's unbearable. Everyone sits
and doesn't even look out of the window. When it's light,
they read. They take care not to let the books slip from
their knees. I had to be careful, not to touch them with my
elbows. They leave their books open when it gets dark. I
listened, I listened in the tunnels, to hear if they shut their
books. I heard nothing. When it was light again, I looked
at the books first and then at their eyes. The books were
open and their eyes were shut. They opened their eyes after
me. I tell you, Windisch," said the skinner, "I felt proud
every time, because I opened my eyes before them. I can
sense the end of the tunnel. I've got that from Russia,"
said the skinner. He held his hand to his forehead. "I have
never experienced," said the skinner, "so many rattling
nights and so many bright days. At night, in bed, I heard
the tunnels. They roared. Roared like the pit waggons in
the Urals."

The skinner nodded his head. His face lit up. He looked
over his shoulder to the table. He looked, in case his wife
was listening. Then he whispered: "Women, Windisch, I
tell you, there are women there. The way they walk. They
reap faster than the men." The skinner laughed. "It's a pity,"
he said, "that they're Wallachians. They're good in bed, but
they can't cook like our women."

A tin bowl stood on the table. The skinner's wife was whisking an eggwhite in the bowl. "I washed two shirts," she said. "The water was black. That's how dirty it is there. You don't see it, because of the forests."

The skinner looked into the bowl. "At the top, on the highest mountain," he said, "there's a sanatorium. That's where the lunatics are. They walk around behind the fence in blue underpants and thick coats. One of them spends all day looking for fir cones in the grass. He talks to himself. Rudi says he's a miner. He started a strike."

The skinner's wife dipped a finger into the eggwhite. "That's what you get," she said and licked the tip of her finger.

"Another one," said the skinner, "was only in the sanatorium for a week. He's back in the mine again. He had been struck by a car."

The skinner's wife lifted the bowl. "These eggs are old," she said, "the snow is bitter."

The skinner nodded. "You can see the cemeteries from the top," he said, "clinging to the slopes of the mountains."

Windisch laid his hands on the table beside the bowl. He said: "I wouldn't like to be buried there."

The skinner's wife looked absent-mindedly at Windisch's hands. "Yes, it must be nice in the mountains," she said. "Only it's so far from here. We can't get there, and Rudi never comes home."

"Now she's baking cakes again," said the skinner, "and Rudi can't even eat them."

Windisch drew his hands back from the table.

"The clouds hang low over the town," said the skinner. "People walk about among the clouds. Every day there's a thunderstorm. People are struck down by lightning in the fields.

Windisch put his hands in his trouser pockets. He stood up. He went to the door.

"I've brought something with me," said the skinner. "Rudi gave me a little box for Amalie." The skinner pulled open a drawer. He shut it again. He looked in an empty suitcase. The skinner's wife looked in his jacket pockets. The skinner opened the cupboard.

Exhausted, the skinner's wife raised her hands. "We'll look for it," she said. The skinner looked in his trouser pockets. "I had the box in my hand only this morning," he said.

THE CLASP-KNIFE

Windisch is sitting in front of the kitchen window. He's shaving. He's painting white foam across his face. The foam crunches on his cheeks. Windisch spreads the snow around his mouth with the tip of his finger. He looks in the mirror. He can see the kitchen door in it. And his face.

Windisch sees that he has painted too much snow on his face. He sees his mouth lying in the snow. He feels that he can't speak because of the snow in his nostrils and the snow on his chin.

Windisch opens the clasp-knife. He tests the blade of the knife against his finger. He places the blade under his eye. His cheekbone doesn't move. With his other hand Windisch pulls flat the wrinkles under his eye. He looks out of the window. He sees the green grass.

The clasp-knife jerks. The blade burns.

Windisch has a wound under his eye for many weeks. It's red. It has a soft edge of pus. And every evening there's plenty of flour dust in it.

A crust has been growing under Windisch's eye for several days.

Each morning, Windisch leaves the house with the crust. When he unlocks the mill door, when he has put the padlock in his pocket, Windisch touches his cheek. The crust has gone.

"Perhaps the crust is lying in the pot hole," he thinks.

When it's light outside, Windisch goes to the mill pond. He kneels down in the grass. He looks at his face in the water. Small circles eddy in his ear. His hair disturbs the picture.

Windisch has a crooked, white scar under his eye.

A reed is bent. It opens and closes beside his hand. The reed has a brown blade.

THE TEAR

Amalie came out of the skinner's yard. She walked through the grass. She held the small box in her hand. She smelt it. Windisch saw the hem of Amalie's dress. It threw a shadow onto the grass. Her calves were white. Windisch saw how Amalie swayed her hips.

The box was tied with silver string. Amalie stood in front of the mirror. She looked at herself. She looked for the silver string in the mirror and tugged at it. "The box was lying in the skinner's hat," she said.

White tissue paper rustled in the box. On the white paper lay a glass tear. It had a hole at its tip. Inside, in its stomach, the tear had a groove. Under the tear lay a note. Rudi had written: "The tear is empty. Fill it with water. Preferably with rainwater."

Amalie couldn't fill the tear. It was summer and the village was parched. And water from the well wasn't rainwater.

Amalie held the tear up to the light at the window. Outside it was hard. But inside, along the groove, it quivered.

For seven days the sky burned itself dry. It had wandered to the end of the village. It looked at the river in the valley. The sky drank water. It rained again.

Water flowed over the paving stones in the yard. Amalie stood by the gutter with the tear. She watched as water flowed into the stomach of the tear.

There was wind in the rainwater too. It drove glassy bells through the trees. The bells were dull; leaves whirled inside them. The rain sang. There was sand in the rain's voice too. And tree-bark.

The tear was full. Amalie brought it into the room with her wet hands and bare, sandy feet.

Windisch's wife took the tear in her hand. Water shone in it. There was a light in the glass. The water from the tear dripped between Windisch's wife's fingers.

Windisch stretched out his hand. He took the tear. The water crawled down his elbow. Windisch's wife licked her wet fingers with the tip of her tongue. Windisch watched as she licked the finger which she had pulled out of her hair on the night of the thunderstorm. He looked out at the rain. He felt the slime in his mouth. A knot of vomit rose in his throat.

Windisch laid the tear in Amalie's hand. The tear dripped. The water in it did not fall. "The water is salty. It burns your lips," said Windisch's wife.

Amalie licked her wrist. "The rain is sweet," she said. "The salt has been wept by the tear."

THE CARRION LOFT

"Schools don't make any difference either," said Windisch's wife.

Windisch looked at Amalie and said: "Rudi's an engineer, but schools don't make any difference either." Amalie laughed.

"Rudi doesn't just know the sanatorium from the outside. He was interned," says Windisch's wife. "The postwoman told me."

Windisch pushed a glass back and forward across the table. He looked into the glass and said: 'It's in the family. They have children, and they're crazy too."

Rudi's great-grandmother was called "the caterpillar" in the village. She always had a thin plait hanging down her back. She couldn't bear a comb. Her husband died young, without falling ill.

After the burial, the caterpillar went looking for her husband. She went to the inn. She looked each man in the face. "It's not you," she said, from one table to the next. The landlord went up to her and said: "But your husband is dead." She held her thin plait in her hand. She wept and ran out into the street.

Every day, the caterpillar went looking for her husband. She went into every house and asked if he had been there.

One winter's day, when the fog was driving white hoops

across the village, the caterpillar went out into the fields. She was wearing a summer dress and no stockings. Only her hands were dressed for snow. She was wearing thick woollen gloves. She walked through the bare thickets. It was late afternoon. The forester saw her. He sent her back to the village.

The next day the forester came into the village. The caterpillar had lain down on a blackthorn bush. She had frozen to death. He brought her into the village across his shoulder. She was as stiff as a board.

"That's how irresponsible she was," said Windisch's wife. "She left her three-year-old child alone in the world." The three-year-old child was Rudi's grandfather. He was a joiner. He didn't care about his fields.

"He let burdock grow on that good soil," said Windisch.

All Rudi's grandfather thought about was wood. He spent all his money on wood. "He made figures out of wood," said Windisch's wife. "He carved faces out of every piece of wood – they were quite monstrous."

"Then came the expropriation," said Windisch. Amalie was painting red nail varnish on her fingernails. "All the farmers were shaking with fear. Some men came from town. They surveyed the fields. They wrote down the names of the people and said: 'Anyone who doesn't sign, will be imprisoned.' All the gates on the lane were locked," said Windisch. "The old skinner didn't lock his gate. He left it wide open.

When the men had come, he said: 'I'm glad you're taking it. Take the horses too, then I'm rid of them.'"

Windisch's wife snatched the bottle of nail varnish out of Amalie's hand. "No one else said that," she said. In her anger, a small blue vein swelled up behind her ear. "Are you listening at all," she had shouted.

The old skinner had carved a naked woman out of the lime tree in the garden. He put it in the yard in front of the window. His wife wept. She took the child. She laid it in a wicker basket. "She took the child and the few things she could carry and moved into an empty house at the edge of the village," said Windisch.

"The child already had a deep hole in its head from all the wood," said Windisch's wife.

The child is the skinner. As soon as he could walk, he went into the fields every day. He caught lizards and toads. When he was bigger, he crept up the church tower at night. He took the owls that couldn't fly out of their nests. He carried them home under his shirt. He fed the owls with lizards and toads. When they were fully grown, he killed them. He hollowed them out. He put them in slaked lime. He dried them and stuffed them.

"Before the war," said Windisch, "the skinner won a goat at the fair. He skinned the goat alive in the middle of the village. Everyone ran away. The women were sick."

"Even today no grass grows on the spot," said Windisch's wife, "where the goat bled to death."

Windisch leant against the cupboard. "He was never a hero," sighed Windisch. "He just knackered animals. We weren't fighting lizards and toads in the war."

Amalie was combing her hair in the mirror.

"He was never in the SS," said Windisch's wife, "only in the army. After the war he started hunting owls and storks and blackbirds again and stuffing them. And he slaughtered all the sick sheep and hares in the district. And tanned the hides. His whole loft is full of carrion."

Amalie reached out for the small bottle of nail varnish.

Windisch felt a grain of sand behind his forehead; it moved from one temple to the other. A red drop fell onto the tablecloth from the small bottle. "You were a whore in Russia," said Amalie to her mother, looking at her fingernail.

THE STONE IN THE LIME

The owl flies in a circle over the apple tree. Windisch looks at the moon. He's watching which direction the black patches are moving. The owl doesn't close its circle.

The skinner had stuffed the last owl from the church tower two years before and given it to the priest as a gift. "This owl lives in another village," thinks Windisch.

The unknown owl always finds its way here to the village

at night. No one knows where it rests its wings by day. No one knows where it closes its beak and sleeps.

Windisch knows that the owl can smell the stuffed birds in the skinner's loft.

The skinner had given the stuffed animals to the town museum as a gift. He didn't receive any money for them. Two men came. Their car stood in front of the skinner's house for a whole day. It was white and closed like a room.

The men said: "These stuffed animals are part of the wildlife population of our forests." They packed all the birds in boxes. They threatened a heavy punishment. The skinner presented them with all his sheepskins. Then they said everything was all right.

The white, closed car drove out of the village as slowly as a room. The skinner's wife smiled in fear and waved.

Windisch is sitting on the veranda. "The skinner applied later than we did," he thinks. "He paid in town."

Windisch hears a leaf on the stones in the hallway. It's scratching on the stones. The wall is long and white.

Windisch closes his eyes. He feels the wall growing on his face. The lime burns his forehead. A stone in the lime opens its mouth. The apple tree trembles. Its leaves are ears. They listen. The apple tree drenches its green apples.

THE APPLE TREE

Before the war an apple tree had stood behind the church. It was an apple tree that ate its own apples.

The night watchman's father had also been night watchman. One summer night he was standing behind the boxwood hedge. He saw the apple tree open a mouth at the top of the trunk, where the branches forked. The apple tree ate apples.

In the morning the night watchman didn't lie down to sleep. He went to the village mayor. He told him that the apple tree behind the church ate its own apples. The mayor laughed. The night watchman could hear fear behind the laughter. Little hammers of life were beating in the mayor's head.

The night watchman went home. He lay in bed with his clothes on. He fell asleep. He slept covered in sweat.

While he was sleeping, the apple tree rubbed the mayor's temple raw. His eyes were reddened and his mouth was dry.

After lunch the mayor struck his wife. He had seen apples floating in the soup. He swallowed them.

The mayor couldn't sleep after his meal. He shut his eyes and heard tree-bark scraping against the other side of the wall. The strips of bark hung in a row. They hung on ropes and ate apples.

That evening the mayor called a meeting. The people assembled. The mayor set up a committee to watch over the apple tree. Four wealthy peasants, the priest, the village teacher and the mayor himself belonged to the committee.

The village teacher made a speech. He named the apple-tree committee the "Summer Night's Committee". The priest refused to mount watch on the apple tree behind the church. He made the sign of the cross three times. He excused himself with: "May God forgive his sinners." He threatened to go into town the following morning and report the blasphemy to the bishop.

Darkness fell very late that evening. The sun had been so hot that the day would not end. Night flowed out of the earth and over the village.

The Summer Night's Committee crawled along the box-wood hedge in the darkness. It lay down under the apple tree, and looked into the tangle of branches.

The mayor had an axe. The wealthy peasants laid their pitchforks in the grass. The village teacher sat under a sack beside a storm lantern with a pencil and an exercise book. He looked through a thumb-sized hole in the sack with one eye, and wrote the report.

The night had reached its peak. It pressed the sky out of the village. It was midnight. The Summer Night's Committee stared at the half-dispersed sky. Under the sack the teacher looked at his pocket watch. Midnight had passed. The church clock had not struck.

The priest had stopped the church clock. Its cogged wheels were not to mark the hour of the sin. Silence was to accuse the village.

No one in the village slept. Dogs stood in the streets, without barking. Cats sat in the trees, looking with glowing lantern eyes.

People sat in their rooms. Mothers carried their children back and forward between burning candles. The children did not cry.

Windisch had sat under the bridge with Barbara.

The teacher had noted the middle of the night on his pocket watch. He stretched out his hand from under the sack. He signalled to the Summer Night's Committee.

The apple tree didn't move. The mayor cleared his throat because of the long silence. One of the wealthy peasants was shaken by a smoker's cough. He quickly picked a tuft of grass. He put the grass in his mouth. He stifled his cough.

Two hours after midnight the apple tree began to tremble. At the top, where the branches forked, a mouth opened. The mouth ate apples.

The Summer Night's Committee heard the mouth gnashing. Behind the wall, in the church, crickets were chirping.

The mouth ate its sixth apple. The mayor ran to the tree. He struck the mouth with his axe. The wealthy peasants raised their pitchforks in the air. They placed themselves behind the mayor.

A piece of bark – yellow and wet – fell into the grass.

The apple tree closed its mouth.

Not one of the Summer Night's Committee had seen how and when the apple tree had closed its mouth.

The teacher crawled out of his sack. As a teacher he must have seen it, the mayor said.

At four o'clock in the morning the priest, wearing his long black cassock, beneath his big black hat, his black briefcase at his side, walked to the station. He walked quickly. Looking down at the ground. Dawn stood on the walls of the houses. The whitewash was light.

Three days later the bishop came to the village. The church was full. The people saw him walking between the benches to the altar. He climbed up to the pulpit.

The bishop didn't pray. He said that he had read the teacher's report. That he had consulted with God. "God has known for a long time," he cried, "God reminded me of Adam and Eve. God," said the bishop softly, "God has told me: 'The devil is in the apple tree.'"

The bishop had written a letter to the priest. He wrote the letter in Latin. The priest read the letter from the pulpit. The Latin made the pulpit seem very high.

The night watchman's father said he hadn't heard the priest's voice.

When the priest had finished reading the letter, he

closed his eyes. He clasped his hands together and prayed in Latin. He climbed down from the pulpit. He seemed small. His face was tired. He turned to face the altar. "We must not fell the tree. We must burn it where it stands," he said.

The old skinner would have been happy to buy the tree from the priest. But the priest said: "God's word is sacred. The bishop knows what to do."

That evening the men brought a waggonload of straw. The four wealthy peasants bound the trunk with straw. The mayor stood on the ladder. He spread straw where the branches forked.

The priest had stood behind the apple tree, praying loudly. The church choir stood alongside the boxwood hedge, singing long songs. It was cold and the breath of the songs was drawn up to the sky. The women and children prayed quietly.

The teacher lit the straw with a burning wood chip. The flame ate the straw. It grew. The flame swallowed the bark of the tree. The fire crackled in the wood. The crown of the tree licked at the sky. The moon covered itself.

The apples puffed up. They burst. The juice hissed, and whined in the fire like living flesh. The smoke stank. It stung the eyes. The songs were broken by coughing.

The village stood in the haze, until the first rain came. The teacher wrote in his exercise book. He called the haze "apple fog".

THE WOODEN ARM

For a long time a humped black stump stood behind the church.

People said that a man was standing behind the church. He looked like the priest without his hat.

Each morning dew fell. The boxwood hedge was sprinkled with white. The stump was black.

The sacristan took the faded roses from the altars and carried them outside behind the church. He passed the stump. The stump was his wife's wooden arm.

Charred leaves whirled around. There was no wind. The leaves were weightless. They rose to his knees. They fell before his steps. The leaves crumbled. They were soot.

The sacristan took the faded roses from the altars and carried them outside the church. He passed the stump. The stump was his wife's wooden arm.

A handful of ashes lay on the ground.

The sacristan put the ashes in a box. He went to the edge of the village. He scraped a hole in the earth with his hands. There was a crooked branch in front of his face. It was a wooden arm. It reached out to him.

The sacristan buried the box in the hole. He walked along a dusty path into the fields. He could hear the trees from far away. The maize had withered. Leaves broke wherever he went. He felt all the loneliness of the years.

His life was transparent. Empty.

Crows flew over the maize. They settled on the maize stalks. They were made of coal. They were heavy. The maize stalks swayed. The crows flapped.

When the sacristan was back in the village, he felt his heart hanging naked and stiff between his ribs. The box with the ashes lay beside the hedge.

THE SONG

The neighbour's spotted pigs are grunting loudly. They are a herd in the clouds. They pass over the house. The veranda is caught in a web of leaves. Each leaf has a shadow.

A man's voice is singing in the sidestreet. The song floats through the leaves. "The village is very large at night," thinks Windisch, "and its end is everywhere."

Windisch knows the song: "Once I travelled to Berlin, the beautiful town to see. Tirihaholala all night long." When it is so dark, when the leaves have shadows, the veranda grows upwards. It presses up under the stones. On a prop. When it has grown too high, the prop breaks. The veranda falls to the ground. Back to where it was. When day comes, no one sees that the veranda has grown and fallen.

Windisch feels the pressure on the stones. There's an

empty table in front of him. Terror is standing on the table. The terror is between Windisch's ribs. Windisch feels the terror hanging like a stone in his jacket pocket.

The song floats through the apple tree: "Send to me your daughter do, for I wish to fuck her now. Tirihaholala all night long."

Windisch pushes a cold hand into his jacket pocket. There is no stone in his jacket pocket. The song is between his fingers. Windisch sings along softly: "Sir, that will not do at all, my daughter dear will not be fucked. Tirihaholala all night long."

The clouds trail over the village, because the herd of pigs in the clouds is so large. The pigs are silent. The song is alone in the night: "Mother mine, allow me please, why then do I have a hole. Tirihaholala all night long."

The way home is long. The man is walking in the dark. The song has no end. "Oh mother dear, do lend me thine, for mine it is so very small. Tirihaholala all night long." The song is heavy. The voice is deep. There is a stone in the song. Cold water is running over the stone. "Oh, I cannot lend it you, for your father needs it soon. Tirihaholala all night long."

Windisch pulls his hand out of his jacket pocket. He loses the stone. He loses the song.

"When she walks," thinks Windisch, "Amalie's toes point outwards when she puts her feet on the ground."

THE MILK

When Amalie was seven years old, Rudi pulled her through the maize. He pulled her to the end of the garden. "The maize is a forest," he said. Rudi took Amalie into the barn. He said: "The barn is a castle."

There was an empty wine-barrel in the barn. Rudi and Amalie crawled into the wine-barrel. "The barrel is your bed," said Rudi. He put dry burs on Amalie's hair. "You have a crown of thorns," he said. "You are enchanted. I love you. You must suffer."

Rudi's pockets were full of shards of coloured glass. He laid the shards around the edge of the barrel. The shards gleamed. Amalie sat down on the floor of the barrel. Rudi knelt in front of her. He pushed up her dress. "I'm drinking milk from you," said Rudi. He sucked Amalie's nipples. Amalie closed her eyes. Rudi bit into the small, brown knots.

Amalie's nipples were swollen. Amalie cried. Rudi went through the end of the garden and into the fields. Amalie ran into the house.

The burs stuck in her hair. They were tangled up. Windisch's wife cut the knots out with her scissors. She washed Amalie's nipples with camomile tea. "You mustn't play with him again," she said. "The skinner's son is crazy. He has a deep hole in his head from all the stuffed animals."

Windisch shook his head. "Amalie will bring disgrace down on us," he said.

THE GOLDEN ORIOLE

There were grey cracks between the blinds. Amalie had a temperature. Windisch couldn't sleep. He was thinking about her chewed nipples.

Windisch's wife sat down on the edge of the bed. "I had a dream," she said. "I went up to the loft. I had the flour sieve in my hand. There was a dead bird on the steps up to the loft. It was a golden oriole. I lifted the bird up by the feet. Under it was a clump of fat, black flies. The flies flew up in a swarm. They settled in the flour sieve. I shook the sieve in the air. The flies didn't move. Then I tore open the door. I ran into the yard. I threw the sieve with the flies into the snow."

THE CLOCK ON THE WALL

T he skinner's windows have fallen into the night. Rudi is lying on his coat, sleeping. The skinner is lying on a coat with his wife, sleeping.

Windisch sees the white patch of the clock on the wall. He sees it on the empty table. A cuckoo lives in the clock. It feels the hour hand. It calls. The skinner gave the clock to the militiaman as a present.

Two weeks ago the skinner showed Windisch a letter. The letter was from Munich. "My brother-in-law lives there," the skinner said. He laid the letter on the table. With the tip of his finger he looked for the lines he wanted to read out. "You should bring your crockery and cutlery with you. Spectacles are expensive here. Fur coats are very expensive." The skinner turned over.

Windisch hears the cuckoo's call. It can smell the stuffed birds through the ceiling. The cuckoo is the only living bird in the house. Its cry breaks up time. The stuffed birds stink.

Then the skinner laughed. He pointed to a sentence at the bottom of the letter. "The women here are worth nothing," he read. "They can't cook. My wife has to slaughter the landlady's hens. The lady refuses to eat the blood or liver. She throws away the stomach and spleen. Apart from that she smokes all day and lets any man at her."

"The worst Swabian woman," said the skinner, "is still worth more than the best German woman from there."

SPURGE LAUREL

The owl no longer calls. It has settled on a roof. "Widow Kroner must have died," thinks Windisch.

Last summer, Widow Kroner plucked linden blossom from the cooper's tree. The tree stands on the left-hand side of the churchyard. Grass grows there. Wild narcissi bloom in the grass. There's a pool in the grass. Around the pool are the graves of the Romanians. They're flat. The water drags them under the earth.

The cooper's linden smells sweet. The priest says that the graves of the Romanians don't belong in the churchyard. That the graves of the Romanians smell different from the graves of the Germans.

The cooper used to go from house to house. He had a sack with many small hammers. He hammered hoops onto barrels. He was given food in return. He was allowed to sleep in the barns.

It was autumn. One could see the coldness of winter through the clouds. One morning the cooper did not wake up. No one knew who he was. Where he came from. "Someone like that is always on the move," the people in the village said.

The branches of the lime tree hang down onto the grave. "You don't need a ladder," said Widow Kroner. "You don't get dizzy." She sat on the grass and plucked the blossom into a basket.

All winter long Widow Kroner drank linden blossom tea. She emptied cups of it into her mouth. Widow Kroner became addicted to the tea. Death was in the cups.

Widow Kroner's face shone. People said: "Something is blooming in Widow Kroner's face." Her face was young. Its youthfulness was weakness. As one grows young before dying, so was her face. As one grows younger and younger, until the body breaks. Beyond birth.

Widow Kroner always sang the same song. "By the well at the gate there stands a lime tree." She added new verses to it. She sang linden blossom verses.

When Widow Kroner drank the tea without sugar, the verses became sad. She looked in the mirror while she sang. She saw the linden blossoms in her face. She could feel the wounds on her stomach and on her legs.

Widow Kroner picked spurge laurel in the fields. She boiled it. She rubbed her wounds with the brown juice. The wounds grew larger and larger. They smelt sweeter and sweeter.

Widow Kroner had picked all the spurge laurel from the fields. She boiled more and more spurge laurel and made more and more tea.

THE CUFFLINKS

Rudi was the only German in the glass factory. "He's the only German in the whole district," said the skinner. "At first the Romanians were amazed that there were still Germans after Hitler. 'Still Germans,' the manager's secretary had said, 'still Germans. Even in Romania.'"

"It has its advantages," the skinner thought. "Rudi earns a lot of money in the factory. He has a good relationship with the man from the secret police. A big blond man with blue eyes. He looks like a German. Rudi says that he's highly educated. He knows all the different kinds of glass. Rudi gave him a glass tie-pin and cufflinks. It paid off," said the skinner. "The man helped us a lot with the passport."

Rudi gave the man all the glass objects he had in his flat. Glass flower pots. Combs. A rocking chair of blue glass. Glass cups and plates. Glass pictures. A glass night light with a red shade.

The ears, the lips, the eyes, the fingers, the toes of glass Rudi brought home in a suitcase. He laid them on the floor. He laid them in rows and circles. He looked at them.

THE CRYSTAL VASE

Amalie is a kindergarten teacher in town. She comes home every Saturday. Windisch's wife waits for her at the station. She helps her carry the heavy bags. Every Saturday, Amalie brings a bag of food and a bag with glass. "Crystal glass," she says.

The cupboards are full of crystal glass. The glass is arranged according to colour and size. Red wineglasses, blue wineglasses, white schnapps glasses. On the tables are glass fruit bowls, vases and flower baskets.

"Presents from the children," says Amalie, when Windisch asks: "Where did you get the glass from?"

For a month Amalie has been talking about a crystal floor vase. She points from the floor to her hips. "That's how tall it is," says Amalie. "It's dark red. On the vase is a dancer in a white lace dress."

Windisch's wife's eyes grow large when she hears about the crystal vase. Every Saturday she says: "Your father will never understand what a crystal vase is worth."

"Ordinary vases used to be good enough," says Windisch. "Now people need floor vases."

Windisch's wife talks about the crystal vase when Amalie is in town. Her face smiles. Her hands become soft. She lifts her fingers into the air as if to stroke someone's cheek. Windisch knows she would spread her legs for a crystal vase. She would spread her legs, just as she strokes the air softly with her fingers.

Windisch becomes hard, when she talks about the crystal vase. He thinks about the years after the war. "In Russia she spread her legs for a piece of bread," the people in the village said after the war.

At the time Windisch thought: "She is beautiful, and hunger hurts."

AMONG THE GRAVES

Windisch had come back to the village from being a prisoner of war. The village was raw from the many dead and wounded.

Barbara had died in Russia.

Katharina had returned from Russia. She wanted to marry Josef. Josef had died in the war. Katharina's face was pale. Her eyes were deep.

Like Windisch, Katharina had seen death. Like Windisch, Katharina had held on to life. Windisch quickly tied his life to her.

Windisch had kissed her on his first Saturday in the stricken village. He pressed her against a tree. He felt her young stomach and her round breasts. Windisch walked through the gardens with her.

The gravestones stood in white rows. The iron gate creaked. Katharina crossed herself. She wept. Windisch knew that she was weeping for Josef. Windisch shut the gate. He wept. Katharina knew that he was weeping for Barbara. Katharina sat down in the grass behind the chapel. Windisch bent down to her. She grasped his hair. She smiled. He pushed up her skirt. He unbuttoned his trousers. He laid himself on her. Her fingers clutched the grass. She panted. Windisch looked up past her hair. The gravestones were bright. She trembled.

Katharina sat up. She smoothed her skirt over her knees. Windisch stood in front of her and buttoned up his trousers. The churchyard was large. Windisch knew that he hadn't died. That he was home. That this pair of trousers had waited for him here in the village, in the wardrobe. That in the war and as a prisoner, he hadn't known where the village was and how long he would continue to live.

Katharina had a stalk of grass in her mouth. Windisch pulled her by the hand. "Let's get away from here," he said.

THE COCKS

The bells of the church strike five times. Windisch feels cold knots in his legs. He goes into the yard. Above the fence, the night watchman's hat passes by. Windisch goes to the gate. The night watchman is holding on tightly to the telegraph pole. He's talking to himself. "Where is she, where has she gone, the fairest of roses?" he says. The dog is sitting on the ground. It's eating a worm.

Windisch says, "Konrad." The night watchman looks at him. "The owl is sitting behind the stack of straw in the meadow," he says. "Widow Kroner is dead." He yawns. His breath smells of schnapps.

The cocks crow in the village. Their cries are harsh. The night is in their beaks.

The night watchman steadies himself against the fence. His hands are dirty. His fingers are bent.

THE DEATH MARK

Windisch's wife stands barefoot on the stone floor of the hallway. Her hair is dishevelled, as if there were a wind in the house. Windisch sees the goosepimples on her calves. The raw skin on her ankles.

Windisch smells her night shirt. It's warm. Her cheek-bones are hard. They twitch. Her mouth tears open. "What time do you call this?" she shouts. "I looked at the clock at three. Now it's already struck five." She waves her hands about in the air. Windisch looks at her finger. It's not slimy.

Windisch crushes a dry apple leaf in his hand. He hears his wife shouting in the hall. She slams the doors. She goes into the kitchen shouting. A spoon clatters on the stove.

Windisch is standing at the kitchen door. She lifts the spoon. "Fornicator," she shouts. "I'll tell your daughter what you get up to."

There's a green bubble above the teapot. Above the bubble is her face. Windisch goes up to her. Windisch strikes her in the face. She says nothing. She lowers her head. Crying, she places the teapot on the table.

Windisch sits in front of the tea cup. The steam eats his face. The peppermint steam drifts into the kitchen. Windisch sees his eye in the tea. The sugar trickles from the spoon into his eye. The spoon stands in the tea.

Windisch drinks a mouthful of tea. "Widow Kroner has died," he says. His wife blows into the cup. She has small red eyes. "The bell is ringing," she says.

There's a red mark on her cheek. It is the mark of Windisch's hand. It is the mark of steam from the tea. It is the death mark of Widow Kroner.

The bell rings through the walls. The lamp rings. The ceiling rings. Windisch breathes deeply. He finds his breath at the bottom of the cup.

"Who knows, when and where we die," says Windisch's wife. She clutches at her hair. She works another strand loose. A drop of tea runs down her chin.

Grey light dawns on the street. The skinner's windows are bright. "The funeral takes place this afternoon," says Windisch.

THE LETTERS

Windisch is riding to the mill. His bicycle tyres squeak in the wet grass. Windisch watches the wheel turning between his knees. The fences drift past in the rain. The trees are dripping. The gardens rustle.

The war memorial is swathed in grey. The small roses have brown edges.

The pot hole is full of water. It drowns the bicycle tyre. Water splashes on Windisch's trouser legs. Earthworms wriggle on the cobblestones.

One of the joiner's windows is open. The bed is made. It's covered with a red plush bedspread. The joiner's wife is sitting alone at the table. A pile of green beans lies on the table.

The lid of Widow Kroner's coffin is no longer leaning against the wall. The joiner's mother smiles from the picture above the bed. Her smile stretches from the death of the white dahlia to the death of Widow Kroner.

The floor is bare. The joiner has sold the red carpets. He has the big form now. He's waiting for the passport.

The rain falls on the back of Windisch's neck. His shoulders are wet.

Sometimes the joiner's wife is summoned to the priest because of the baptismal certificate, sometimes to the militiaman because of the passport.

The night watchman has told Windisch that the priest has an iron bed in the sacristy. In this bed he looks for baptismal certificates, with the women. "If things go well," said the night watchman, "he looks for the baptismal certificates five times. If he's doing the job thoroughly, he looks ten times. With some families the militiaman loses and mislays the applications and the revenue stamps seven times. He looks for them on the mattress in the post office store room with the women who want to emigrate."

The night watchman laughed. "Your wife," he said to Windisch, "is too old for him. He'll leave your Kathi in peace. But then it'll be your daughter's turn. The priest makes her Catholic, and the militiaman makes her stateless. The postwoman gives the militiaman the key when he's got work to do in the store room."

Windisch kicked the mill door with his foot. "Let him try," he said. "He may get flour, but he won't get my daughter."

"That's why our letters don't arrive," said the night watchman. "The postwoman takes the envelopes from us and money for the stamps. She buys schnapps with the money for the stamps. And she reads the letters and throws them into the wastepaper basket. And if the militiaman doesn't have any work to do in the store room, he sits behind the counter with the postwoman and swigs schnapps. Because the postwoman is too old for him and the mattress."

The night watchman stroked his dog. "The postwoman has already drunk away hundreds of letters," he said. "And has read the militiaman hundreds of letters."

Windisch unlocks the mill door with the big key. He counts two years. He turns the small key in the lock. Windisch counts the days. Windisch walks to the mill pond.

The surface of the pond is disturbed. There are waves on it. The willows are wrapped in leaves and wind. The stack of straw throws its moving, everlasting picture on the pond. Frogs crawl round the stack. They drag their white bellies through the grass.

The night watchman is sitting beside the pond and has hiccups. His larynx bounces out of his shirt. It's the blue onions," he says. "The Russians cut thin slices off the top of onions. They sprinkle salt on them. The salt makes the onions open like roses. They give off water. Clear, bright water. They look like water lilies. The Russians hit them with their fists. I've seen Russians crush onions under their heels. The women lifted their skirts and knelt on the onions. They turned their knees. We soldiers held the Russian women at the hips and helped them turn."

The night watchman had watery eyes. "I've eaten onions that were tender and sweet as butter from the knees of Russian women," he says. His cheeks are flabby. His eyes grow young as the sheen of onions.

Windisch carries two sacks to the edge of the pond. He covers them with canvas. The night watchman will take them to the militiaman during the night.

The reeds are quivering. White foam sticks to the blades. "That's what the dancer's lace dress must be like," thinks Windisch. "I'm not letting a crystal vase into my house."

"There are women everywhere. There are even women in the pond," says the night watchman. Windisch sees their underclothes among the reeds. He goes into the mill.

THE FLY

Widow Kroner lies in the coffin, dressed in black. Her hands are tied together with a white cord, so that they don't slide down from her stomach. So that they are praying, when she arrives up above, at heaven's gate.

"She's so beautiful, it's as if she were asleep," says her neighbour, Skinny Wilma. A fly settles on her hand. Skinny Wilma moves her finger. The fly settles on a small hand beside her.

Windisch's wife shakes the raindrops from her headscarf.

They fall in transparent chains onto her shoes. Umbrellas stand beside the praying women. Water snakes and trickles under the chairs. It glistens among the shoes.

Windisch's wife sits down on the empty chair beside the door. She cries a large tear out of each eye. The fly settles on her cheek. The tear rolls down onto the fly. It flies into the room, the edge of its wing damp. The fly returns. It settles on Windisch's wife. On her wrinkled index finger.

Windisch's wife prays and looks at the fly. The fly creeps all round the fingernail. It tickles her skin. "It's the fly that was under the golden oriole. The fly that settled in the flour sieve," thinks Windisch's wife.

Windisch's wife finds a moving passage in the prayer. She sighs over the passage. She sighs and her hands move. And the fly on her fingernail feels the sigh. And it flies past her cheek into the room.

Windisch's wife's lips softly hum, pray for us.

The fly flies just below the ceiling. It hums a long song for the death vigil. A song of rainwater. A song of the earth as a grave.

Windisch's wife forces out two more small tears as she hums. She lets them run down her cheek. She lets them grow salty around her mouth.

Skinny Wilma looks for her handkerchief. She looks among the shoes. Between the rivulets that crawl out of the black umbrellas.

Skinny Wilma finds a rosary among the shoes. Her face

is pointed and small. "Whose rosary is it?" she asks. No one looks at her. Everyone is silent. "Who knows," she sighs, "there have already been so many here."

She puts the rosary in the pocket of her long black skirt.

The fly settles on Widow Kroner's cheek. A living thing on her dead skin. The fly buzzes in the still corner of her mouth. The fly dances on her hard chin.

Outside the window, the sound of rain. The prayer leader bats her short eyelashes as if the rain was running into her face. As if it was washing away her eyes. Eyelashes which are broken from praying. "A cloudburst," she says. "Over the whole country." She closes her mouth even while she's talking, as if the rain was running down into her throat.

Skinny Wilma looks at the dead woman. "Only in the Banat," she says. "Our weather comes from Austria, not from Bucharest."

The water lingers on the streets. Windisch's wife sniffles away a last small tear. "The old people say that anyone whose coffin it rains into was a good person," she says to the room.

There are bunches of hydrangea above Widow Kroner's coffin. They are wilting, heavy and violet. Death, skin and bones, lying in the coffin is taking them. And the prayer of the rain is taking them.

The fly crawls into the scentless hydrangea buds.

The priest comes through the door. His step is heavy, as

if his body was full of water. The priest gives the altar boy
the black umbrella and says, "Jesus Christ be praised." The
women hum, and the fly hums.

The joiner brings the coffin lid into the room.

A hydrangea leaf trembles. Half violet, half dead, it
falls onto the praying hands joined by the white cord. The
joiner lays the coffin lid on the coffin. He nails the coffin
shut with black nails and short hammer blows.

The hearse gleams. The horse looks at the trees. The
coachman lays the grey blanket across the horse's back.
"The horse will catch cold," he says to the joiner.

The altar boy holds the large umbrella over the priest's
head. The priest has no legs. The hem of his black cassock
trails in the mud.

Windisch feels the water gurgling in his shoes. He
knows the nail in the sacristy. He knows the long nail on
which the cassock hangs. The joiner steps in a puddle.
Windisch watches his laces drown.

"The black cassock has already seen a lot," thinks
Windisch. "It has seen the priest looking for baptismal
certificates on the iron bed with women." The joiner asks
something. Windisch hears his voice. Windisch doesn't
understand what the joiner is saying. Windisch hears the
clarinet and the big drum behind him.

Rain fringes the brim of the night watchman's hat.
The shroud flaps on the hearse. The bunches of hydrangea
quiver in the pot holes. They strew leaves in the mud. The

mud glistens under the wheels. The hearse turns in the glass puddle.

The music is cold. The big drum sounds dull and wet. Above the village, the roofs are leaning towards the water.

The cemetery glows with white crosses. The bell hangs over the village with its stuttering tongue. Windisch sees his hat in the puddle. "The pond will grow," he thinks. "The rain will pull the militiaman's sacks into the water."

There's water in the grave. The water is yellow like tea. "Widow Kroner can drink now," whispers Skinny Wilma.

The prayer leader steps on a marguerite lying on the path between the graves. The altar boy holds the umbrella at an angle. The incense is drawn into the earth.

The priest lets a handful of mud drip onto the coffin. "Earth, take what is thine. God takes what is his," he says. The altar boy sings a long wet "Amen". Windisch can see his back teeth.

Water eats at the shroud. The night watchman is holding his hat against his chest. He's crushing the brim in his hand. The hat is wrinkled. The hat is rolled up like a black rose.

The priest closes his prayerbook. "We shall meet again on the other side," he says.

The gravedigger is a Romanian. He leans the shovel against his stomach. He makes the sign of the cross on his shoulders. He spits in his hands. He shovels.

The band plays a cold funeral song. The song has no

end. The tailor's apprentice blows into his French horn. He has white spots on his blue fingers. He glides into the song. The big yellow horn is by his ear. It shines like the horn of a gramophone. The funeral song explodes as it tumbles out of the horn.

The big drum booms. The prayer leader's throat hangs between the ends of her headscarf. The grave fills with earth.

Windisch closes his eyes. They hurt from the wet, white marble crosses. They hurt from the rain.

Skinny Wilma goes out by the churchyard gate. Bunches of hydrangea lie broken in Widow Kroner's grave. The joiner stands at his mother's grave and weeps.

Windisch's wife is standing on the marguerite. "Let's go," she says. Windisch walks beside her under the black umbrella. The umbrella is a large black hat. Windisch's wife is carrying the hat on a stick.

The gravedigger stands barefoot and alone in the churchyard. He's cleaning his rubber boots with the shovel.

THE KING IS SLEEPING

Before the war the village band had stood at the station in their dark red uniforms. The station gable was hung with garlands of tiger-lilies, China asters and acacia foliage.

People were wearing their Sunday clothes. The children wore white knee socks. They held heavy bouquets of flowers in front of their faces.

When the train steamed into the station, the band played a march. People clapped. The children threw their flowers in the air.

The train moved slowly. A young man stretched his long arm out of the window. He spread his fingers and called: "Silence. His Majesty the King is sleeping."

When the train had left the station, a herd of white goats came from the meadow. They went along the tracks and ate the bouquets of flowers.

The musicians had gone home with their interrupted march. The men and women had gone home with their interrupted waving. The children had gone home with empty hands.

A little girl who was to have recited a poem for the King when the march had finished, when the clapping had finished, sat in the waiting room and cried, until the goats had eaten all the bunches of flowers.

A BIG HOUSE

The cleaning woman wipes the dust from the banisters. She has a black mark on her cheek and a violet eye. She's crying: "He hit me again," she says.

The clothes hooks shine empty around the walls of the hallway. They are a thorny garland. The slippers, small and worn down, stand in a perfect row beneath the hooks.

Each child has brought a transfer to the nursery from home. Amalie stuck the little pictures under the hooks.

Every morning each child looks for its car, its dog, its doll, its flower, its ball.

Udo comes through the door. He's looking for his flag. It is black, red and gold. A German flag. Udo hangs his coat on the hook, above the flag. He takes off his shoes. He puts on his red slippers. He places his shoes under his coat.

Udo's mother works in the chocolate factory. Every Tuesday she brings Amalie sugar, butter, cocoa and chocolate. "Udo will only be coming to the nursery for another three weeks," she said to Amalie yesterday. "We've been told about our passport."

The dentist pushes her daughter through the half-open door. A white beret hangs on the girl's hair like a snowflake. The girl looks for her dog among the hooks. The dentist gives Amalie a bunch of carnations and a small box. "Anca has a cold," she says. "Please give her the tablets at ten o'clock."

The cleaning woman shakes the duster out of the window. The acacia is yellow. The old man sweeps the pavement in front of his house as he does every morning. The leaves of the acacia are blown by the wind.

The children are wearing their Falcons' uniforms. Yellow blouses and dark blue trousers and pleated skirts. "It's Wednesday," Amalie thinks, "Falcons' day."

Building bricks click. Cranes buzz. Indians march in columns in front of little hands. Udo is building a factory. Dolls are drinking milk from little girls' fingers.

Anca's forehead is hot.

The anthem can be heard through the classroom ceiling. The big group is singing on the floor above.

The building blocks are lying on top of one another. The cranes are silent. The column of Indians stands at the edge of the table. The factory has no roof. The doll with the long silk dress is lying on the chair. She's sleeping. She has a rosy face.

The children stand in a semi-circle in front of the teacher's desk in order of size. They press the palms of their hands against their thighs. They raise their chins. Their eyes grow large and wet. They sing loudly.

The boys and girls are little soldiers. The anthem has seven verses.

Amalie hangs the map of Romania on the wall.

"All children live in blocks of flats or in houses," says Amalie. "Every house has rooms. All the houses together make one big house. This big house is our country. Our fatherland."

Amalie points at the map. "This is our Fatherland," she says. With her fingertip she searches for the black dots on the map. "These are the towns of our Fatherland," says Amalie. "The towns are the rooms of this big house, our country. Our fathers and mothers live in our houses. They are our parents. Every child has its parents. Just as the father in the house in which we live is our father, so Comrade Nicolae Ceauşescu is the father of our country. And just as the mother in the house in which we live is our mother, so Comrade Elena Ceauşescu is the mother of our country. Comrade Nicolae Ceauşescu is the father of all the children. And Comrade Elena Ceauşescu is the mother of all the children. All the children love Comrade Nicolae and Comrade Elena, because they are their parents."

The cleaning woman leaves an empty wastepaper basket by the door. "Our fatherland is called the Socialist Republic of Romania," says Amalie. "Comrade Nicolae Ceauşescu is the General Secretary of our country, the Socialist Republic of Romania."

A boy stands up. "My father has a globe at home," he says. He shapes a globe with his hands. A hand knocks against a vase. The carnations are lying in the water. His Falcons' shirt is wet.

Shards of glass are lying on the little table in front of him. He's crying. Amalie pushes the little table away from him. She must not shout. Claudiu's father is the manager of the butcher's shop at the corner.

Anca lays her face on the table. "When can we go home?" she asks in Romanian. German is cumbersome and passes her by. Udo is building a roof. "My father is the general secretary of our house," he says.

Amalie looks at the yellow leaves of the acacia. The old man leans out of the open window, as he does every day. "Dietmar is buying cinema tickets," thinks Amalie.

The Indians march across the floor. Anca swallows the pills.

Amalie leans against the window frame. "Does anyone know a poem?" she asks.

"I know a land with an arc of mountains,/ On whose peaks early glows the morning,/ In whose woods as through the ocean waves/ The spring wind roars till all is blooming."

Claudiu speaks German well. Claudiu raises his chin. Claudiu speaks German with the voice of a shrunken grown man.

TEN LEI

The little gypsy girl from the next village is wringing out her grass-green apron. Water runs from her hand. Her plait hangs down onto her shoulder from the middle of her head. A red ribbon is plaited into her hair. It sticks out at the end like a tongue. The little gypsy girl stands barefoot with muddy toes in front of the tractor drivers.

The tractor drivers are wearing small, wet hats. Their black hands are on the table. "Show me," says one. "I'll give you ten lei." He puts ten lei on the table. The tractor drivers laugh. Their eyes gleam. Their faces are red. Their glances finger the long flowery skirt. The gypsy girl lifts her skirt. The tractor driver empties his glass. The gypsy girl takes the bank note from the table. She twists the plait around her finger and laughs.

Windisch can smell the schnapps and the sweat from the next table. "They wear their sheepskins all summer long," says the joiner. Froth from his beer clings to his thumbs. He dips his forefinger into the glass. "The dirty pig beside us is blowing ash into my beer," he says. He looks at the Romanian standing behind him. The Romanian has a cigarette in the corner of his mouth. It's wet from his saliva. He laughs.

"No more German," he says. Then in Romanian: "This is Romania."

The joiner has a greedy look. He raises his glass and empties it. "You'll soon be rid of us," he shouts. He signals to the landlord, who is standing at the tractor driver's table. "Another beer," he calls.

The joiner wipes his mouth with the back of his hand. "Have you been to the gardener yet?" he asks.

"No," says Windisch. "Do you know where he lives?" asks the joiner. Windisch nods: "On the edge of town." "In Fratelia, in Enescu Street," says the joiner.

The little gypsy girl pulls at the red tongue of her plait. She laughs and turns in a circle. Windisch sees her calves. "How much?" he asks.

"Fifteen thousand each," says the joiner. He takes the glass of beer from the landlord's hand. "A single-storey building. The greenhouses are on the left. If the red car is in the courtyard, it's open. There'll be someone cutting wood in the yard. He'll take you into the house," says the joiner. "Don't ring. If you do, the woodcutter will disappear. He won't open up anymore."

The men and women standing in the corner of the inn are drinking out of a bottle. A man wearing a crushed, black velveteen hat is holding a child in his arm. Windisch sees the small, naked soles of the child's feet. The child reaches for the bottle. It opens its mouth. The man pushes the neck of the bottle to its mouth. The child closes its eyes and drinks. "Boozer," says the man. He pulls back the bottle and laughs. The woman beside him is eating a crust of bread. She chews and drinks. White breadcrumbs float in the bottle.

"They stink of the sty," says the joiner. A long brown hair hangs from his finger.

"They're from the dairy," says Windisch.

The women sing. The child totters up to them and tugs at their skirts.

"Today's pay day," says Windisch. "They drink for three days. Then they've got nothing left."

"The milkmaid with the blue headscarf lives behind the mill," says Windisch.

The little gypsy girl lifts her skirt. The gravedigger is standing beside his shovel. He reaches into his pocket. Gives her ten lei.

The milkmaid with the blue headscarf sings and vomits against the wall.

THE SHOT

The conductress's sleeves are rolled up. She's eating an apple. The second-hand on her watch twitches. It's five past. The tram squeals.

A child pushes Amalie over an old woman's suitcase. Amalie hurries.

Dietmar is standing at the entrance to the park. His

mouth is hot on Amalie's cheek. "We've got time," he says. "The tickets are for seven. Five o'clock is sold out."

The bench is cold. Small men carry wicker baskets full of dead leaves across the grass.

Dietmar's tongue is hot. It burns Amalie's ear. Amalie shuts her eyes. Dietmar's breath is bigger in her head than the trees. His hand is cold under her blouse.

Dietmar closes his mouth. "I've got my call-up papers for the army," he says. "My father's brought my suitcase."

Amalie pushes his mouth away from her ear. She presses her hand over his mouth. "Come into town," she says, "I'm cold."

Amalie leans against Dietmar. She feels his steps. She nestles under his jacket as though she were part of him.

There's a cat in the shop window. It's sleeping. Dietmar knocks on the pane. "I still have to buy some woollen socks," he says. Amalie eats a roll. Dietmar blows a cloud of smoke into Amalie's face.

"Come on," says Amalie, "I'll show you my crystal vase."

The dancer lifts her arm above her head. The white lace dress is stiff behind the window pane.

Dietmar opens a wooden door at the side of the shop. Behind the door is a dark passageway. The darkness smells of rotten onions. Three rubbish bins stand like big tins in a row against the wall.

Dietmar pushes Amalie onto the bin. The lid rattles.

Amalie feels Dietmar's thrusting member in her stomach. She holds on tightly to his shoulders. A child is talking in the inner courtyard.

Dietmar buttons his trousers. Music is coming out of the small window at the back of the yard.

Amalie sees Dietmar's shoes moving forward in the queue. A hand tears the tickets in half. The usherette is wearing a black headscarf and a black dress. She switches off her torch. Corn cobs trickle out of the long neck of the harvester behind the tractor. The short is over.

Dietmar's head rests on Amalie's shoulder. Red letters appear on the screen: "Pirates of the Twentieth Century." Amalie puts her hand on Dietmar's knee. "Another Russian film," she whispers.

Dietmar lifts his head. "At least it's in colour," he says in her ear.

The green water ripples. Green forests line the shore. The deck of the ship is wide. A beautiful woman is holding on to the ship's railing. Her hair blows like leaves.

Dietmar crushes Amalie's finger in his hand. He looks at the screen. The beautiful woman speaks.

"We won't see each other again," he says. I've got to join the army, and you're emigrating." Amalie sees Dietmar's cheek. She moves. She speaks. "I've heard Rudi's waiting for you," says Dietmar.

On the screen, a hand opens. It reaches into a jacket pocket. On the screen are a thumb and an index finger.

Between them is a revolver.

Dietmar is talking. Behind his voice, Amalie hears the shot.

WATER HAS NO PEACE

"The owl is injured," says the night watchman. "A cloud-burst on the day of a funeral is too much even for an owl. If it doesn't see the moon tonight, it won't ever fly again. If it dies, the water will stink."

"The owls have no peace, and the water has no peace," says Windisch. "If it dies, another owl will come to the village. A stupid young owl that doesn't know anything. It will sit on anyone's roof."

The night watchman looks up at the moon. "Then young people will die again," he says. Windisch sees that the air just in front of him belongs to the night watchman.

His voice manages a tired sentence. "Then it will be like the war again," he says.

"The frogs are croaking in the mill," says the night watchman.

They make the dog crazy.

THE BLIND COCK

Windisch's wife sits on the edge of the bed. "There were two men here today," she says. "They counted the hens and noted it down. They caught eight hens and took them away. They put them in wire cages. The trailer on their tractor was full of hens." Windisch's wife sighs. "I signed," she says. "And for four hundred kilos of maize and a hundred kilos of potatoes. They'll take those later, they said. I gave them the fifty eggs right away. They went into the garden in rubber boots. They saw the clover in front of the barn. Next year we'll have to grow sugar-beet there, they said."

Windisch lifts the lid from the pot. "And next door?" he asks. "They didn't go there," says Windisch's wife. She gets into bed and covers herself up. "They said that our neighbours have eight small children, and we have one, and she's earning money."

There is blood and liver in the pot. "I had to kill the big white cock," says Windisch's wife. "The two men were running about in the yard. The cock took fright. He flapped up against the fence and struck his head against it. When they had left he was blind."

Onion rings float on eyes of fat in the pot. "And you said we'll keep the big white cock so we'll get big white hens next year," says Windisch.

"And you said anything white is too sensitive. And you were right," says Windisch's wife.

The cupboard creaks.

"When I was riding to the mill, I got off at the war memorial," says Windisch in the dark. "I wanted to go into the church and pray. The church was locked. I thought, that's a bad sign. Saint Anthony is on the other side of the door. His thick book is brown. It's like a passport."

In the warm, dark air of the room, Windisch dreams that the sky opens up. The clouds fly away out of the village. A white cock flies through the empty sky. It strikes its head against a bare poplar standing in the meadow. It can't see. It's blind. Windisch stands at the edge of a sunflower field. He calls out: "The bird is blind." The echo of his voice returns as his wife's voice. Windisch goes deep into the sunflower field and shouts: "I'm not looking for you, because I know you aren't here."

THE RED CAR

The wooden hut is a black square. Smoke creeps out of a tin pipe. It creeps into the damp earth. The door of the hut is open. A man in blue overalls is sitting on a wooden bench inside the hut. A tin bowl is lying on the table. It's steaming. The man's eyes follow Windisch.

The manhole cover has been pushed aside. A man is standing in the drain. Windisch sees his head with its yellow helmet above ground. Windisch walks past the man's chin. The man's eyes follow Windisch.

Windisch puts his hands in his coat pockets. He feels the wad of money in the inside pocket of his jacket.

The greenhouses are on the left side of the courtyard. The panes are misted up. The mist swallows the branches. Roses burn red in the vapour. The red car stands in the middle of the yard. There are logs beside the car. Chopped wood is piled up against the wall of the house. The axe lies beside the car.

Windisch walks slowly. He crushes the tram ticket in his coat pocket. He feels the wet asphalt through his shoes.

Windisch looks round. The woodcutter is not in the courtyard. The head with the yellow helmet looks at Windisch.

The fence ends. Windisch hears voices in the next house. A garden gnome is dragging a hydrangea shrub. It's wearing a red cap. A snow-white dog is running round in a circle and barking. Windisch looks down the street. The rails run on into emptiness. Grass grows between the rails. The blades of grass are black from oil, small and bent from the creaking tram and the screaming rails.

Windisch turns round. The yellow helmet ducks into the drain. The man in the blue overalls leans a brush against the side of the shed. The garden gnome is wearing a green apron. The hydrangea shrub trembles. The snow-white dog stands silently by the fence. The snow-white dog follows Windisch with its eyes.

Smoke billows out of the hut's tin pipe. The man in the blue overalls brushes up the mud around the shed. His eyes follow Windisch.

The windows of the house are shut. The white curtains make him blind. Two rows of barbed wire are stretched between rusty hooks along the top of the fence. The stack of wood has white ends. It's freshly cut. The blade of the axe glints. The red car stands in the middle of the yard. The roses bloom in the misty vapour.

Windisch walks past the chin of the man with the yellow helmet again.

The barbed wire ends. The man in the blue overalls is sitting in the hut. He follows Windisch with his eyes.

Windisch turns round. He stands by the gate.

Windisch opens his mouth. The head with the yellow helmet is above the ground. Windisch shivers. He has no voice in his mouth.

The tramcar rumbles. Its windows are misted up. The conductor follows Windisch with his eyes.

The bell is on the doorpost. It has a white fingertip. Windisch presses it. It rings in his finger. It rings in the yard. It rings far away inside the house. On the far side of the walls, the ringing is muffled as if buried.

Windisch presses the white fingertip fifteen times.

Windisch counts. The shrill notes in his finger, the loud notes in the yard, the notes buried in the house all flow into one another.

The gardener is buried in the glass, in the fence, in the walls.

The man in the blue overalls rinses out the tin bowl. He looks. Windisch walks past the chin of the man in the yellow helmet. Windisch follows the rails with the money in his jacket.

Windisch's feet are sore from the asphalt.

THE SECRET WORD

Windisch rides home from the mill. Noon is bigger than the village. The sun scorches its path. The pot hole is cracked and dry.

Windisch's wife is sweeping the yard. Sand lies around her toes like water. The ripples around the broom are still. "It's not yet autumn, and the acacias are turning yellow," says Windisch's wife.

Windisch unbuttons his shirt. "It's going to be a hard winter," he says, "if the trees are already dry in the summer."

The hens turn their heads under their wings. With their beaks they're seeking out their own shadows, which offer no cool. The neighbour's spotted pigs root among the wild, white-flowering carrots behind the fence. Windisch looks through the wire. "They don't give these pigs anything to eat," he says. "Wallachians. They don't even know how to feed pigs."

Windisch's wife holds the broom to her stomach. "They should have rings in their noses," she says. "They'll root up the house by the time winter comes."

Windisch's wife carries the broom into the shed. "The postwoman was here," she says. "She belched and stank of schnapps. The militiaman thanks you for the flour, she said, and Amalie should come for the hearing on Sunday morning. She should bring an application with her and sixty lei's worth of revenue stamps."

Windisch bites his lip. His mouth expands into his face, into his forehead. "What good are thanks?" he says.

Windisch's wife raises her head. "I knew it," she says, "you won't get far with your flour."

"Far enough," shouts Windisch into the yard "for my daughter to become a mattress." He spits in the sand: "It's disgusting, the shame of it." A drop of saliva hangs on his chin.

"You won't get far with 'it's disgusting' either," says Windisch's wife. Her cheekbones are two red stones. "It's not a question of shame now," she says, "it's a question of the passport."

Windisch slams the door shut. "You should know,"

he shouts, "you should know from Russia. You weren't bothered about shame then."

"You pig," cries Windisch's wife. The shed door opens and shuts, as if the wind was in the wood. Windisch's wife searches for her mouth with a fingertip. "When the militiaman sees that our Amalie is still a virgin, he won't want to do it," she says.

Windisch laughs. "A virgin like you were a virgin, in the churchyard after the war," he says. "People starved to death in Russia, and you lived from whoring. And after the war you would have gone on whoring, if I hadn't married you."

Windisch's wife lets her mouth fall open. She raises her hand. She raises her forefinger into the air. "You make everybody bad," she shouts, "because you're no good yourself and not right in the head either." She walks across the sand. Her heels are full of cuts.

Windisch follows her heels. She stops on the veranda. She lifts her apron and wipes the empty table with the apron. "You did something wrong at the gardener's," she says. "Everybody is let in. Everybody sees about their passport. Except you, because you're so clever and honest."

Windisch goes into the hall. The refrigerator hums. "There was no electricity all morning," says Windisch's wife. "The refrigerator defrosted. The meat will go off if this continues."

There's an envelope on the refrigerator. "The

postwoman brought a letter," says Windisch's wife. "From the skinner."

Windisch reads the letter. "Rudi isn't mentioned in the letter," says Windisch. "He must be back in the sanatorium."

Windisch's wife looks into the yard. "He sends greetings to Amalie. Why doesn't he write himself?"

"He wrote this sentence here," says Windisch. "This sentence with PS." Windisch lays the letter on the refrigerator.

"What does PS mean?" asks Windisch's wife.

Windisch shrugs. "It must be a secret word."

Windisch's wife stands in the doorway. "That's what happens when children study," she sighs.

Windisch stands in the yard. The cat is lying on the paving stones. It's asleep. It's lying in the sun. Its face is dead. The stomach breathes weakly beneath the fur.

Windisch sees the skinner's house, caught in the midday light. The sun gives it a yellow radiance.

THE PRAYER HOUSE

"The skinner's house is going to become a prayer house for the Wallachian Baptists," says the night watchman to Windisch in front of the mill. "The ones with small hats are Baptists. They howl when they pray. And their women groan when they sing hymns, as if they were in bed. Their eyes get big, like my dog's."

The night watchman is whispering, although only Windisch and his dog are by the pond. He's looking into the night, in case a shadow comes to listen and look. "They're all brothers and sisters," he says. "On their festival days they pair off. With whoever they catch in the dark."

The night watchman follows a water rat with his eyes. The rat cries with a child's voice and throws itself into the reeds. The dog doesn't hear the night watchman's whispers. It stands at the edge and barks at the rat.

"They do it on the carpet in the prayer house," says the night watchman. "That's why they have so many children."

Windisch feels a burning salty sneeze in his nose and forehead from the pond water and the whispering of the night watchman. And Windisch has a hole in his tongue. From being astounded and staying silent.

"This religion comes from America," says the night watchman. Windisch breathes through his salty sneeze. "That's across the water."

"The devil crosses the water too," says the night watchman. "They've got the devil in their bodies. My dog can't stand them either. He barks at them. Dogs can scent the devil."

The hole in Windisch's tongue slowly fills up. "The

skinner always said," says Windisch, "that the Jews run America."

"Yes," says the night watchman, "the Jews are the ruin of the world. Jews and women."

Windisch nods. He's thinking of Amalie. "Every Saturday, when she walks home," he thinks, "I have to look and see how her toes point outwards when she puts her feet on the ground."

The night watchman eats a third green apple. His jacket pocket is full of green apples. "It's true about the women in Germany," says Windisch. "That's what the skinner wrote. The worst one here is still worth more than the best one there."

Windisch looks at the clouds. "Women there follow the latest fashions," says Windisch. "They would prefer to walk naked on the street if they could. The skinner says, even schoolchildren read magazines full of naked women."

The night watchman rummages among the green apples in his jacket pocket. The night watchman spits out a bite. "There have been worms in the fruit since the cloudburst," he says. The dog licks the spat-out piece of apple. It eats the worm.

"There's something rotten about this whole summer," says Windisch. "My wife sweeps the yard every day. The acacias are withering. There are none in our yard. The Wallachians have three in their yard. They are far from bare. And every day there are enough yellow leaves in our yard for ten trees. My wife doesn't know where all the leaves are coming from. There have never been so many dry leaves in our yard before."

"The wind brings them," says the night watchman. Windisch locks the mill door.

"There isn't any wind," he says.

The night watchman holds a finger in the air: "There's always wind, even if one doesn't feel it."

"In Germany the forests are drying up in the middle of the year too," says Windisch.

"The skinner told us," he says. He looks at the broad, low sky. "They've settled in Stuttgart. Rudi's in another town. The skinner doesn't write where. The skinner and his wife have been given a subsidized flat with three rooms. They have a kitchen with a dining area and a bathroom with mirrored walls."

The night watchman laughs. "At their age they still like looking at themselves naked in the mirror," says the night watchman.

"Some rich neighbours have given them furniture," says Windisch. "And a television as well. Their next-door neighbour is a woman who lives by herself. She's a squeamish old lady, says the skinner, she doesn't eat any meat. It would be the death of her, she says."

"They've got it too easy," says the night watchman "They should come to Romania, then they'll eat anything."

"The skinner has a good pension," says Windisch. "His

wife is a cleaner in an old people's home. The food there is good. When one of the old people has a birthday they have a dance."

The night watchman laughs. "That would be the life for me," he says. "Good food and a few young women."

He bites into the core of his apple. The white pips fall onto his jacket. "I don't know," he says, "I can't make up my mind whether to apply."

Windisch sees time standing still in the night watchman's face. Windisch sees the end on the night watchman's cheeks, and he sees that the night watchman will stay there beyond the end.

Windisch looks at the grass. His shoes are white with flour. "Once you've started," he says, "things just keep going."

The night watchman sighs. "It's difficult if you're alone," he says. "It takes a long time and we're not getting any younger."

Windisch puts his hand on his trouser leg. His hand is cold, and his thigh is warm. 'It's getting worse and worse here," he says. "They're taking our hens, our eggs. They take our maize too, before it even ripens. They'll take your house too and the holding."

The moon is large. Windisch can hear the rats going into the water. "I feel the wind," he says. "The knots in my legs are sore. It must be going to rain soon."

The dog is beside the stack of straw and barking. "The

wind from the valley doesn't bring rain," says the night watchman, "only dust and clouds."

"Perhaps a storm is coming," says Windisch, "which will bring the fruit down from the trees again."

The moon has a red veil.

"And Rudi?" asks the night watchman.

"He's taking a rest," says Windisch. He can feel the lie burning on his cheeks. "In Germany it's not like here with glass. The skinner writes that we should bring our crystal glass with us. Our porcelain, and feathers for the pillows. But not damask and underwear. They've got them there in abundance. Furs are very expensive. Furs and spectacles."

Windisch chews a blade of grass. "The beginning isn't easy," says Windisch.

Windisch ties the blade of grass around his forefinger. "One thing is hard, says the skinner in his letter. An illness we all know from the war. Homesickness."

The night watchman holds an apple in his hand. "I wouldn't feel homesick," he says. "After all, you're among Germans there."

Windisch ties knots in the blade of grass. "There are more foreign nations there than here, says the skinner. There are Turks and Negroes. They're increasing rapidly," says Windisch.

Windisch pulls the blade of grass through his teeth. The

blade of grass is cold. His gums are cold. Windisch holds the sky in his mouth. The wind and the night sky. The blade of grass shreds between his teeth.

THE CABBAGE WHITE

A malie is standing in front of the mirror. Her slip is pink. White lace points show under Amalie's navel. Windisch sees the skin above Amalie's knee through the holes in the lace. There are fine hairs on Amalie's knee. Her knee is white and round. Windisch sees Amalie's knee in the mirror yet again. He sees the holes in the lace run into one another.

Windisch's wife's eyes are in the mirror. The tips of Windisch's eyelashes are beating fast, driving into his temples. A red vein swells in the corner of Windisch's eye. It tears the tips from the lashes. A torn tip moves in the pupil of Windisch's eye.

The window is open. The leaves on the apple tree are reflected in the panes.

Windisch's lips are burning. They're saying something.

But he's only talking to himself, to the walls. Inside his own head.

"He's talking to himself," says Windisch's wife in the mirror.

A cabbage white flies through the window into the room. Windisch follows it with his eyes. Its flight is flour and wind.

Windisch's wife reaches into the mirror. With flabby fingers she straightens the straps of the slip on Amalie's shoulder.

The cabbage white flutters over Amalie's comb. Amalie pulls the comb through her hair with an elongated arm. She blows away the cabbage white with its flour. It alights on the mirror. It staggers over the glass, across Amalie's stomach.

Windisch's wife presses her fingertip against the glass. She squashes the cabbage white on the mirror.

Amalie sprays two large clouds under her armpits. The clouds run down beneath her arms and into the slip. The spray can is black. In bright green letters on the can are the words Irish Spring.

Windisch's wife hangs a red dress across the back of the chair. She places a pair of white sandals with high heels and narrow straps under the chair. Amalie opens her handbag. She dabs on eyeshadow with her fingertip. "Not too much," says Windisch's wife, "otherwise people will talk." Her ear is in the mirror. It's large and grey. Amalie's eyelids are pale blue. Amalie's mascara is made of soot. Amalie pushes her face very close to the mirror. Her upward glance is made of glass.

A strip of tinfoil falls out of Amalie's handbag onto the

carpet. It is full of round white warts. "What's that you've got?" asks Windisch's wife.

Amalie bends down and puts the strip back in her bag. "The pill," she says. She twists the lipstick out of its black holder.

Windisch's wife puts her cheekbones in the mirror. "What do you need pills for?" she asks. "You're not ill."

Amalie pulls the red dress over her head. Her forehead slips through the white collar. Her eyes still under the dress, Amalie says: "I take it just in case."

Windisch presses his hand against his forehead. He leaves the room. He sits down on the veranda, at the empty table. The room is dark. It is a shadowy hole in the wall. The sun crackles in the trees. Only the mirror shines. Amalie's red mouth is in the mirror.

Small, old women are walking past the skinner's house. The shadow of their black headscarves precedes them. The shadow will be in church before the small, old women.

Amalie walks over the cobblestones on her white heels. She holds the square, folded application in her hand like a white briefcase. Her red dress swings around her calves. The Irish Spring flies into the yard. Amalie's dress is darker beneath the apple tree than in the sun.

Windisch sees that Amalie's toes point outwards as she puts her feet on the ground.

A strand of Amalie's hair flies over the alley gate. The gate snaps shut.

MASS

Windisch's wife is standing in the yard behind the black grapes. "Aren't you going to mass?" she asks. The grapes grow out of her eyes. The green leaves grow out of her chin.

"I'm not leaving the house," says Windisch, "I don't want people saying to me: now it's your daughter's turn."

Windisch puts his elbows on the table. His hands are heavy. Windisch puts his face in his heavy hands. The veranda doesn't grow. It's broad daylight. For a moment the veranda falls to a place where it never was before. Windisch feels the blow. A stone hangs in his ribs.

Windisch closes his eyes. He feels his eyes. He feels his eyeballs in his hands. His eyes without a face.

With naked eyes and with the stone in his ribs, Windisch says loudly: "A man is nothing but a pheasant in the world." What Windisch hears is not his voice. He feels his naked mouth. It's the walls that have spoken.

THE BURNING GLOBE

The neighbour's spotted pigs are lying in the wild carrots, sleeping. The black women come out of the church. The sunshine is bright. It lifts them over the pavement in their small, black shoes. Their hands are worn from the rosaries. Their gaze is still radiant from praying.

Above the skinner's roof the church bell strikes the middle of the day. The sun is a great clock above the midday tolling. Mass is over. The sky is hot.

Behind the small, old women the pavement is empty. Windisch looks along the houses. He sees the end of the street. "Amalie should be coming," he thinks. There are geese in the grass. They are white like Amalie's white sandals.

The tear lies in the cupboard. "Amalie didn't fill it," thinks Windisch. "Amalie's never at home when it rains. She's always in town."

The pavement moves in the light. The geese sail along. They have white sails in their wings. Amalie's snow-white sandals don't walk through the village.

The cupboard door creaks. The bottle gurgles. Windisch holds a wet, burning globe on his tongue. The globe rolls down his throat. A fire flickers in Windisch's temples. The globe dissolves. It draws hot threads through Windisch's forehead. It pushes crooked furrows like partings through his hair.

The militiaman's cap circles round the edge of the mirror. His epaulettes flash. The buttons of his blue jacket grow larger in the centre of the mirror. Windisch's face appears above the militiaman's jacket.

First Windisch's face appears large and confident above the jacket. Then Windisch's face is small and dejected above the epaulettes. The militiaman laughs between the cheeks of Windisch's large, confident face. With wet lips he says: "You won't get far with your flour."

Windisch raises his fists. The militiaman's jacket shatters. Windisch's large, confident face has a spot of blood. Windisch strikes the two small, despondent faces above the epaulettes dead.

Windisch's wife silently sweeps up the broken mirror.

THE LOVE BITE

Amalie stands in the doorway. There are red spots on the slivers of glass. Windisch's blood is redder than Amalie's dress.

The last breath of Irish Spring hangs on Amalie's calves. The love bite on Amalie's neck is redder than her dress. Amalie pulls off her white sandals. "Come and eat," says Windisch's wife.

The soup is steaming. Amalie sits in its fog. She holds the spoon with her red fingertips. She looks at the soup. The steam moves her lips. She blows. Sighing, Windisch's wife sits down in the grey cloud that rises from her plate.

The leaves on the trees rustle through the windows.

"They're blowing into the yard," thinks Windisch. "There are enough leaves for ten trees blowing into the yard."

Windisch looks past Amalie's ear. It's part of what he can see. Reddish and creased like an eyelid.

Windisch swallows a soft white noodle. It sticks in his throat. Windisch puts his spoon on the table and coughs. His eyes fill with water.

Windisch brings up the soup into his plate. His mouth tastes sour. It rises to his brow. The soup in Windisch's plate is cloudy from the vomit.

Windisch can see a large courtyard in the soup. It's a summer evening in the courtyard.

THE SPIDER

That Saturday Windisch had danced through the night with Barbara in front of the deep horn of the gramophone. They talked about the war as they waltzed.

A paraffin lamp flickered under the quince tree. It stood on a chair.

Barbara had a thin neck. Windisch danced with her thin neck. Barbara had a pale mouth. Windisch hung on her breath. He swayed. The swaying was a dance.

Under the quince tree, a spider had fallen into Barbara's hair. Windisch didn't see the spider. He leant against

Barbara's ear. He heard the song on the gramophone through her thick black plait. He felt her hard comb.

By the paraffin lamp, Barbara's green clover leaves shone from both ears. Barbara whirled in a circle. The whirling was a dance.

Barbara felt the spider on her ear. She started. Barbara cried: "I'm dying."

The skinner danced in the sand. He danced past. He laughed. He took the spider from Barbara's ear. He threw it in the sand. He stamped on it with his shoe. The stamping was a dance.

Barbara had leant against the quince tree. Windisch held her head.

Barbara's hand went to her ear. The green clover leaf no longer hung on her ear. Barbara didn't look for it. Barbara didn't dance any more. She wept. "I'm not weeping for the earring," she said.

Later, many days later, Windisch had sat with Barbara on a bench in the village. Barbara had a thin neck. One green clover leaf shone. The other ear was dark in the night.

Windisch shyly asked about the second earring. Barbara looked at him. "Where would I have looked for it?" she said. "The spider took it away to the war. Spiders eat gold."

After the war, Barbara followed the spider. The snow in Russia took her away, when it melted the second time.

THE LETTUCE LEAF

Amalie licks a chicken bone. The lettuce crunches in her mouth. Windisch's wife holds a chicken wing to her mouth. "He's drunk all the schnapps," she says. She sucks at the yellow skin. "Out of grief."

Amalie pricks a lettuce leaf with the prong of her fork. She holds the leaf to her mouth. She speaks and the leaf trembles. "You won't get far with your flour," she says. Her lips hold the lettuce leaf tight like a caterpillar.

"Men have to drink because they suffer," smiles Windisch's wife. Amalie's eyeshadow is a blue fold over her eyelashes. "And suffer, because they drink," she giggles. She looks through a lettuce leaf.

The love bite on her neck is darker. It's turning blue, and it moves, when she swallows.

Windisch's wife sucks the small, white bones. She swallows the short pieces of meat on the chicken's neck. "Keep your eyes open, when you get married," she says. "Drinking is a bad illness." Amalie licks her red fingertips. "And unhealthy," she says.

Windisch looks at the dark spider. "Whoring is healthier," he says.

Windisch's wife strikes the table with her hand.

GRASS SOUP

Windisch's wife had been in Russia for five years. She had slept in a hut with iron beds. Lice cracked in the edges of the beds. She was shaved. Her face was grey. Her scalp was red-raw.

On top of the mountains there was yet another mountain range of clouds and drifting snow. Frost burned on the truck. Not everyone got off at the mine. Every morning some men and women remained sitting on the benches. They sat with open eyes. They let everyone go past. They were frozen. They were sitting on the other side.

The mine was black. The shovel was cold. The coal was heavy.

When the snow melted the first time, thin, pointed grass grew in the snow stone hollows. Katharina had sold her winter coat for ten slices of bread. Her stomach was a hedgehog. Every day, Katharina picked a bunch of grass. The grass soup was warm and good. The hedgehog pulled in its spines for a few hours.

Then the second snow came. Katharina had a woollen blanket. During the day it was her coat. The hedgehog stabbed.

When it was dark, Katharina followed the light of the snow. She bent down. She crawled past the guard's shadow. Katharina went into a man's iron bed. He was a cook. He called her Kathe. He warmed her and gave her potatoes. They were hot and sweet. The hedgehog pulled in its spines for a few hours.

When the snow melted the second time, grass soup grew beneath their shoes. Katharina sold her woollen blanket for ten slices of bread. The hedgehog pulled in its spines for a few hours.

Then the third snow came. The sheepskin was Katharina's coat.

When the cook died, the light of the snow shone in another hut. Katharina crawled past the shadow of another guard. She went into a man's iron bed. He was a doctor. He called her Katyusha. He warmed her and gave her a white piece of paper. That was an illness. For three days Katharina did not need to go to the mine.

When the snow melted the third time, Katharina sold her sheepskin for a bowl of sugar. Katharina ate wet bread and sprinkled sugar on it. The hedgehog pulled in its spines for a few days.

Then the fourth snow came. The grey woollen socks were Katharina's coat.

When the doctor died, the light of the snow shone over the storeyard. Katharina crawled past the sleeping dog. She went into a man's iron bed. He was the gravedigger. He buried the Russians in the village too. He called her Katja. He warmed her. He gave her meat from the funeral meals in the village.

When the snow melted the fourth time, Katharina sold her grey woollen socks for a bowl of maize flour. The maize porridge was hot. It swelled up. The hedgehog pulled in its spines for a few days.

Then the fifth snow came. Katharina's brown cloth dress was her coat.

When the gravedigger died, Katharina had put on his coat. She crawled through the fence along the snow. She went to an old Russian woman in the village. The grave-digger had buried her husband. The old Russian woman recognized Katharina's coat. It was her husband's coat. Katharina warmed herself in her house. She milked the goats. The Russian woman called her Devochka. She gave her milk.

When the snow melted the fifth time, yellow clusters of flowers bloomed in the yard.

A yellow dust floated in the grass soup. It was sweet.

One afternoon green trucks drove into the storeyard. They crushed the grass. Katharina sat on a stone in front of the hut. She saw the dirty tracks of the tyres. She saw the strange guards.

The women climbed up onto the green trucks. The tyre tracks didn't lead to the mine. The green trucks stopped in front of the little station.

Katharina climbed onto the train. She wept with happiness.

Katharina's hands were sticky with grass soup, when she learned that the train was going home.

THE SEAGULL

Windisch's wife switches on the television. The singer leans against a railing by the sea. The hem of her skirt flutters. The tips of the singer's slip hang above her knee.

A seagull flies over the water. It flies close to the edge of the screen. Its wing tip thrusts into the room.

"I've never been to the seaside," says Windisch's wife. "If the sea wasn't so far away, seagulls would come to the village." The seagull plunges down to the water. It swallows a fish.

The singer smiles. She has the face of a seagull. She opens and closes her eyes as often as her mouth. She sings a song about the girls from Romania. Her hair wants to be water. Small waves ripple at her temples.

"The girls from Romania," sings the singer, "are gentle as the flowers in the meadows in the month of May." Her hands point to the sea. Sandy bushes quiver by the shore.

A man is swimming in the water. He swims after his hands. Far out into the water. He is alone, and the sky ends. His head moves on the surface. The waves are dark.

The seagull is white.

The singer's face is soft. The wind shows the lace hem of her slip.

Windisch's wife stands in front of the screen. She points at the singer's knee with her fingertip. "The lace is nice," she says, "it's definitely not from Romania."

Amalie stands in front of the screen. "The lace dress of the dancer on the crystal vase is exactly like that."

Windisch's wife puts some plain cakes on the table. The tin bowl is under the table. The cat licks the soupy vomit from it.

The singer smiles. She closes her mouth. Behind her song the sea beats on the shore. "Your father should give you money for the crystal vase," says Windisch's wife.

"No," says Amalie. "I've saved some money. I'll pay for it myself."

THE YOUNG OWL

The young owl has been sitting in the valley for a week. People see it every evening when they come back from town. Grey dusk lies over the rails. Strange, black maize waves around the train. The young owl sits among the faded thistles as if in snow.

People get out at the station. They don't speak. The

train hasn't whistled for a week. They hold their bags close to them. They are on their way home. When they meet other people on the way home, they say: "That is the last stopping place. Tomorrow the young owl will be there to catch up on the dying."

The priest sends the altar-boy up into the church tower. The bell peals. When the altar-boy is back down on the ground again, he is pale. "I don't pull the bell. The bell pulls me," he says. "If I hadn't held onto the beam, I would have flown up into the sky."

The pealing of the bell confused the young owl. It flew back into the country. It flew south. Along the Danube. It flew along the sound of the water, to where the soldiers are.

In the south, the plain is treeless and hot. It's burning. The young owl sets its eyes alight among the red hips. With its wings above the barbed wire it wishes itself a death.

The soldiers lie in the grey morning. Thickets separate them. They are on manoeuvres. They are at war with their hands, their eyes, their foreheads.

The officer shouts an order.

A soldier sees the young owl in the thicket. He lays his rifle in the grass. He stands up. The bullet flies. It strikes.

The dead man is the tailor's son. The dead man is Dietmar.

The priest says: "The young owl sat by the Danube and thought of our village."

Windisch looks at his bicycle. He has brought the news of the bullet from the village to the farm. "It's just like in the war again," he says.

Windisch's wife raises her eyebrows. "It's nothing to do with the owl," she says. "It was an accident." She pulls a yellow leaf from the apple tree. She looks Windisch up and down, from his head to his shoes. Looks a long time at the breast pocket of the jacket, under which his heart beats.

Windisch feels the fire in his mouth. "Your understanding is tiny," he shouts. "It doesn't even stretch from your forehead down to your mouth." Windisch's wife cries and crushes the yellow leaf.

Windisch feels the pressure of the grain of sand in his forehead. "She's crying for herself," he thinks. "Not for the dead man. Women only ever cry for themselves."

THE SUMMER KITCHEN

The night watchman is sleeping on the bench in front of the mill. His black hat makes his sleep velvety and heavy. His forehead is a pale streak. "The earth frog is in his head again," thinks Windisch. He sees time standing still on his cheeks.

The night watchman is talking in his dream. His legs twitch. The dog barks. The night watchman wakes up.

Startled, he takes off the hat. His forehead is wet. "She'll kill me," he says. His voice is deep. It goes back into his dream.

"My wife was lying naked and curled up on the pastry board," says the night watchman. "Her body was no larger than the body of a child. Yellow juice was dripping from the pastry board. The floor was wet. There were old women sitting round the table. They were dressed in black. Their plaits were unkempt. They hadn't combed their hair for a long time. Skinny Wilma was as small as my wife. She was holding a black glove in her hand. Her feet didn't reach the floor. She was looking out of the window. Then the glove fell out of her hand. Skinny Wilma looked under the chair. The glove wasn't under the chair. The floor was bare. The floor was so far below her feet that she had to cry. She screwed up her wrinkled face and said: 'It's a disgrace to leave the dead lying there in the summer kitchen.' I said I didn't even know that we had a summer kitchen. My wife raised her head from the pastry board and smiled. Skinny Wilma looked at her. 'Don't mind me,' she said to my wife. And then to me: 'She's dripping and she smells.'"

The night watchman's mouth is open. Tears run down his cheeks.

Windisch grips him by the shoulder. "You're driving yourself crazy," he says. The keys jingle in his jacket pocket.

Windisch pushes the door of the mill with his foot.

The night watchman looks into his black hat. Windisch pushes his bicycle past the bench. "I'm going to get the passport," he says.

THE GUARD OF HONOUR

T he militiaman is standing in the tailor's yard. He's giving schnapps to the officers. He's giving schnapps to the soldiers who carried the coffin into the house. Windisch sees the stars on their epaulettes.

The night watchman leans his face towards Windisch. "The militiaman is happy," he says, "because he's got company."

The mayor is standing under the yellow plum tree. He's sweating. He's looking at a sheet of paper. Windisch says: "He can't read the writing, because the teacher wrote the funeral speech."

"He wants two sacks of flour tomorrow evening," says the night watchman. He smells of schnapps.

The priest comes into the yard. His black coat trails along the ground. The officers quickly shut their mouths. The militiaman puts the bottle of schnapps behind the tree.

The coffin is made of metal. It shines in the yard like a gigantic tobacco tin. The guard of honour carries the coffin out of the yard, their boots faithfully keeping time with the march.

On the truck is a red cloth.

The black hats of the men bob quickly by. The black headscarves of the women pass more slowly behind them. Loosely tied to the black knots of their rosaries. The coachman walks. He talks loudly.

The guard of honour on the truck is tossed from side to side. The soldiers hold on tightly to their rifles because of the pot holes. They are too high above the ground, too high above the coffin.

Widow Kroner's grave is still black and high. "The earth hasn't settled, because it hasn't rained," says Skinny Wilma. The bunches of hydrangea have crumbled away.

The postwoman comes and stands beside Windisch "How nice it would be," she says, "if young people came to the funeral too. It's been like this for years," she says. "When someone in the village dies, none of the young people turn up." A tear falls onto her hand. "Amalie has to come for an interview on Sunday morning."

The prayer leader sings in the priest's ear. The incense distorts her mouth.

She is so transfixed and holy in her singing that the whites of her eyes grow large, sluggishly covering the pupils.

The postwoman sobs. She grips Windisch by the elbow. "And two sacks of flour," she says.

The bell strikes till its clapper is sore. The volleys of the military salute rise above the graves. Heavy clods of earth fall onto the tin coffin.

The prayer leader remains standing at the war memorial. With the corners of her eyes she searches out a place to stand. She looks at Windisch. She coughs. Windisch hears the phlegm breaking in her throat, now emptied of song.

"Amalie is to come to see the priest on Saturday afternoon," she says. "The priest has to look for her baptismal certificate in the register."

Windisch's wife ends the prayer. She takes two steps. She stops in front of the prayer leader's face. "The baptismal certificate isn't so urgent, is it?" she says. "Very urgent," says the prayer leader. "The militiaman has told the priest that your passports are ready at the Passport Office now."

Windisch's wife crushes her handkerchief. "Amalie is bringing a crystal vase on Saturday," she says. "It's fragile."

"She can't go straight to the priest from the station," says Windisch.

The prayer leader grinds the sand with the tip of her shoe. "Then she should go home first," she says. "The days are still long."

GYPSIES BRING LUCK

The kitchen cupboard is empty. Windisch's wife bangs the doors shut. The little gypsy girl from the next village stands barefoot in the middle of the kitchen, where the table used to stand. She puts the cooking-pots into her large sack. She unties her handkerchief. She gives Windisch's wife twenty-five lei. "I don't have any more," she says. The tongue of ribbon sticks out of her plait. "Give me a dress as well," she says. "Gypsies bring luck."

Windisch's wife gives her Amalie's red dress. "Now go," she says. The little gypsy girl points to the teapot. "The teapot too," she says. "I'll bring you luck."

The milkmaid with the blue headscarf pushes the hand-cart with the pieces of the bed through the gate. The old bedding is tied to her back.

Windisch shows the television to the man with the small hat. He switches it on. The screen hums. The man carries the television out. He puts it on the table on the veranda. Windisch takes the banknotes from his hand.

A horse and cart from the dairy are standing in front of the house. A man and woman are standing by the white patch where the bed used to be. They look at the wardrobe and the dressing table. "The mirror is broken," says Windisch's wife. The milkmaid lifts up a chair and looks at the underside of the seat. Her companion taps the table top with his fingers. "The wood is sound," says Windisch. "You can't buy furniture like that in the shops any more."

The room is empty. The cart with the wardrobe goes along the street. The chair legs stick up beside the wardrobe. They rattle like the wheels. The table and dressing table are on the grass outside the house. The milkmaid sits on the grass and follows the cart with her eyes.

The postwoman wraps the curtains in a newspaper. She looks at the refrigerator. "It's been sold," says Windisch's wife. "The tractor man is coming to collect it this evening."

The hens lie with their heads in the sand. Their feet have been tied together. Skinny Wilma is putting them in the wicker basket. "The cock went blind," says Windisch's wife. "I had to kill it." Skinny Wilma counts the banknotes. Windisch's wife holds her hand out for them.

The tailor has black braid on the points of his collar. He rolls up the carpet. Windisch's wife looks at his hands. "You can't escape fate," she sighs.

Amalie looks at the apple tree through the window. "I don't know," says the tailor. "He never harmed a soul."

Amalie feels a sob in her throat. She leans her face out of the window. She hears the shot.

Windisch is standing in the yard with the night watchman. "There's a new miller in the village," says the night watchman. "A Wallachian with a small hat from a water mill." The night watchman hangs some shirts, jackets and trousers over the carrier of the bicycle. He reaches into his pocket. "I said, it's a present," says Windisch.

Windisch's wife tugs at her apron. "Take them," she says, "he's glad to give them to you. There's still a pile of old clothes lying around for the gypsies." She tugs at her cheek. "Gypsies bring luck," she says.

THE SHEEP FOLD

The new miller is standing on the veranda. "The mayor sent me," he says. "I'm going to be living here."

His small hat is at an angle. His sheepskin is new. He looks at the table on the veranda. "I could use that," he says. He walks through the house. Windisch follows him. Windisch's wife follows Windisch barefoot.

The new miller looks at the door in the hall. He turns the handle. He looks at the walls and ceiling in the hall. He knocks on the door. "This door is old," he says. He leans against the door frame and looks into the empty room. "I was told the house was furnished," he says. "What do you mean, furnished?" says Windisch. "I've sold my furniture."

Windisch's wife stamps out of the hall. Windisch can feel his head throbbing.

The new miller looks at the walls and ceiling in the room. He opens and closes the window. He presses the floorboards down with the tip of his shoe. "Then I must phone my wife," says the miller. "She'll have to bring some furniture."

The miller goes into the yard. He looks at the fences. He sees the neighbour's spotted pigs. "I've got ten pigs and twenty-six sheep," he says. "Where's the sheepfold?"

Windisch sees the yellow leaves on the sand. "We've never had sheep," he says. Windisch's wife comes into the yard with a broom in her hand. "The Germans don't have any sheep," she says. The broom crunches lightly in the sand.

"The shed will make a good garage," says the miller. "I'll get hold of some planks and build a sheepfold."

The miller shakes Windisch's hand. "The mill is beautiful," he says.

Windisch's wife brushes large circular waves in the sand.

THE SILVER CROSS

Amalie is sitting on the floor. The wine glasses are lined up according to size. The schnapps glasses are all shiny. The milky flowers on the sides of the fruit bowls are rigid. The vases stand along the wall. The crystal vase stands in the corner of the room.

Amalie holds the small box with the tear in her hand.

Amalie hears the tailor's voice inside her head: "He never harmed a soul."

A piece of fire burns in Amalie's forehead.

Amalie feels the militiaman's mouth on her neck. His breath smells of schnapps. He squeezes her knee with his hand. He pushes her dress up. "*Ce dulce eşti* – You're so sweet," he says. His cap lies beside his shoe. The buttons on his tunic shine.

The militiaman unbuttons his tunic. "Take your clothes off," he says. A silver cross hangs beneath the blue tunic. The priest takes off his black cassock. He brushes a strand of hair from Amalie's cheek. "Wipe your lipstick off," he says. The militiaman kisses Amalie's shoulder. The silver cross falls in front of his mouth. The priest strokes Amalie's thigh. "Take your slip off," he says.

Amalie sees the altar through the open door. Among the roses is a black telephone. The silver cross hangs between Amalie's breasts. The militiaman's hands squeeze Amalie's breasts. "You've got nice apples," says the priest. His mouth is wet. Amalie's hair hangs over the side of the bed. Her white sandals are under the chair. The militiaman whispers: "You smell good." The priest's hands are white. Light catches the red dress at the end of the iron bed. The black telephone rings among the flowers. "I haven't got time now," groans the militiaman. The priest's thighs are heavy. "Cross your legs on my back," he whispers. The silver cross presses into Amalie's shoulder. The militiaman has a damp forehead. "Turn round," he says. The black cassock hangs on the long nail behind the door. The priest's nose is cold. "My little angel," he pants.

Amalie feels the heels of the white sandals in her stomach. The fire from her forehead is burning in her eyes. Amalie's tongue presses down in her mouth. The silver cross gleams in the window pane. A shadow is hanging in the apple tree. It's black and disturbed. The shadow is a grave.

Windisch is standing in the doorway. "Are you deaf?" he says. He holds the big suitcase out to Amalie. Amalie turns her face to the door. Her cheeks are wet. "I know," says Windisch, "leave-taking is hard." He seems very large in the empty room. "It's just like in the war again," he says. "We go and we don't know, if and how and when we'll come back."

Amalie fills the tear once again. "It doesn't get so wet with water from the well," she says. Windisch's wife puts the plates into a suitcase. She takes the tear in her hand. Her cheekbones are soft and her lips are damp. "You would hardly believe, that there is such a thing," she says.

Windisch can feel her voice inside his head. He throws his coat into the suitcase. "I've had enough of her," he shouts, "I don't want to see her any more." He lowers his head. And quietly adds: "The only thing she can do is make people sad."

Windisch's wife wedges the cutlery between the plates.

"Indeed it is," she says. Windisch sees the slimy finger

which she pulled out of her hair. He looks at his passport photo. He rocks his head from side to side. "It's a difficult step," he says.

Amalie's glass shines in her suitcase. The white patches on the walls of the room grow larger. The floor is cold. The light bulb casts long rays into the suitcase.

Windisch puts the passports in his jacket pocket. "Who knows what will become of us?" sighs Windisch's wife. Windisch looks at the piercing rays of light. Amalie and Windisch's wife shut the suitcase.

THE PERM

A wooden bicycle creaks in the fence. Above, a bicycle of white cloud swims peacefully in the sky. Around the white clouds the clouds are water. Grey and empty as a pond. Around the pond only silent mountains. Grey mountain ranges heavy with longing for home.

Windisch is carrying two large suitcases, and Windisch's wife is carrying two large suitcases. Her head is moving too quickly. Her head is too small. The stones of her cheekbones are enclosed in darkness. Windisch's wife has cut off her plait. Her short hair is permed. Her mouth is hard and narrow from her new teeth. She talks loudly.

Box trees sway in the church garden. A strand loosens

from Amalie's hair. The strand returns to her ear.

The pot hole is cracked and grey. The poplar stands like a broom in the sky.

Jesus sleeps on the cross by the church door. When he wakes up, he'll be old. The air in the village will be brighter than his naked skin.

At the post office the lock is hanging on its chain. The key is in the postwoman's house. It opens the lock. It opens the mattress for the hearings.

Amalie is carrying the heavy suitcase with her glass. Her handbag hangs over her shoulder. In it is the box with the tear. In her other hand, Amalie carries the crystal vase with the dancer.

The village is small. People are walking in the side streets. They're far away. And are drawing further away. The maize is a black wall at the end of the streets.

Windisch sees the grey swathes of time standing still around the station platform. A blanket of milk lies over the rails. It reaches up to their heels. Over the blanket lies a glassy skin. The still time spins a web around the suitcases. It tugs at their arms. Windisch shuffles over the gravel.

The steps of the train are high. Windisch lifts his shoes out of the blanket of milk.

Windisch's wife wipes the dust from the seats with her handkerchief. Amalie holds the crystal vase on her knees. Windisch presses his face against the window. A picture of the Black Sea hangs on the wall of the compartment. The water stands still. The picture rocks. It's travelling, too.

"I'll feel sick in the aeroplane," says Windisch. "I know that from the war." Windisch's wife laughs. Her new teeth chatter.

Windisch's suit is too tight. The sleeves are too short. "The tailor made it too small for you," says Windisch's wife. "Such expensive cloth and completely wasted."

As the train travels on, Windisch feels his forehead slowly filling with sand. His head is heavy. His eyes sink into sleep. His hands tremble. His legs twitch and are awake. Windisch sees an expanse of rusty scrub through the window. "Since the owl took his son, the tailor can't think anymore," says Windisch. Windisch's wife holds her chin in her hand.

Amalie's head hangs on her shoulder. Her hair covers her cheeks. She's sleeping. "Let her sleep," says Windisch's wife.

"Now that I don't have my plait anymore, I don't know how to hold my head." Her new dress with the white lace collar shines green like water.

The train rattles over the iron bridge. The sea rocks over the wall of the compartment, over the river. There is much sand but little water in the river.

Windisch follows the beating wings of the small birds. They fly in ragged flocks. They're searching for woods along the river flats, where there are only thickets and sand and water.

The train travels slowly, because the rails criss-cross in confusion, because the town is beginning. Scrap heaps. Small houses stand in overgrown gardens. Windisch sees that many rails run into one another. He sees other trains on the confusion of rails.

The golden cross on the chain hangs over the green dress. There is so much green around the cross.

Windisch's wife moves her arm. The cross swings on the chain. The train travels quickly. It has found an empty track among the many trains.

Windisch's wife stands up. Her gaze is fixed and certain. She sees the station. Under her perm, inside her skull, Windisch's wife has already furnished the new world, into which she is carrying her large suitcase. Her lips are like cold ashes. "God willing, we'll come back for a visit next summer," she says.

The pavement is cracked. The puddles have swallowed the water. Windisch locks the car. A silver circle gleams on the car. Inside it are three spokes like three fingers. There are flies on the bonnet. Bird shit sticks to the windscreen. Behind on the boot, the word Diesel. A horse-drawn waggon rattles by. The horses are bony. The waggon is made of dust. The carter is a stranger. He has large ears under his small hat.

Windisch and Windisch's wife are walking in a ball of cloth. He's wearing a grey suit. She has a grey costume of the same cloth.

Windisch's wife is wearing black shoes with high heels.

In the pot hole Windisch feels the cracks tugging at his shoes. There are blue veins on his wife's white calves.

Windisch's wife looks at the sloping red roofs. "It's as if we never lived here," she says. She says it as if the sloping roofs were red pebbles under her shoes. A tree lays its shadow over her face. Her cheekbones are stony. The shadow withdraws to the tree. It leaves wrinkles on her chin. Her golden cross gleams. The sun catches it. The sun holds its flames on the cross.

The postwoman is standing by the boxwood hedge. There is a tear in her patent leather bag. The postwoman holds out her cheek for a kiss. Windisch's wife gives her a bar of Ritter Sport chocolate. The sky-blue paper is shiny. The postwoman lays her fingers on its golden edge.

Windisch's wife moves the stones in her cheekbones. The night watchman comes towards Windisch. He raises his black hat. Windisch sees his own shirt and his own jacket. The wind drives the shadow of a spot onto Windisch's wife's chin. The shadow falls onto the jacket of her costume. Windisch's wife wears the shadow beside her collar like a dead heart.

"I've got a wife," says the night watchman. "She's a milkmaid in the cowsheds in the valley."

Windisch's wife sees the milkmaid with the blue
headscarf standing outside the inn next to Windisch's
bicycle. "I know her," says Windisch's wife, "she bought
our bed."

The milkmaid looks across the road to the square in
front of the church. She eats an apple and waits.

"I suppose you don't want to emigrate now," says
Windisch. The night watchman crushes his hat in his hands.
He looks over to the inn. "I'm staying here," he says.

Windisch sees the band of dirt on his shirt. A vein beats
on the night watchman's neck. Time stands still. "My wife
is waiting," says the night watchman. He points over to
the inn.

The tailor raises his hat in front of the war memorial.
He looks at the tips of his shoes as he walks. He stops at
the church door beside Skinny Wilma.

The night watchman brings his mouth up to Windisch's
ear. "There's a young owl in the village," he says. "It knows
its way around. It's already made Skinny Wilma ill." The
night watchman smiles. "Skinny Wilma is clever," he says.
"She scared the owl away." He looks over to the inn. "I'm
going," he says.

A cabbage white flutters past the tailor's face. The tailor's
cheeks are pale, like curtains under his eyes.

The cabbage white flies through the tailor's cheek. The
tailor sinks his head. The cabbage white flies out of the back
of the tailor's head, white and uncrumpled. Skinny Wilma

flaps her handkerchief. The cabbage white flies through her forehead and into her head.

The night watchman walks beneath the trees. He pushes Windisch's old bicycle.

The car's silver badge jingles in the night watchman's jacket pocket. The milkmaid walks barefoot in the grass beside the bicycle. Her blue headscarf is a patch of water. Leaves are floating in it.

The prayer leader walks slowly through the church door carrying a thick hymn book. It's St Anthony's book.

The church bell strikes. Windisch's wife is standing at the church door. The organ hums through Windisch's hair in the dark air. Windisch walks down the bare passageway between the benches with his wife. Their heels click on the stone. Windisch's hands are clasped. Windisch is hanging from his wife's golden cross. A tear of glass hangs on his cheek.

Skinny Wilma's eyes follow Windisch. Skinny Wilma lowers her head. "He got that suit from the army," she says to the tailor. "They're taking communion and haven't confessed."

GLOSSARY

Banat Former Hungarian province under the Habsburg monarchy. After the First World War it was divided between Romania and Yugoslavia.

Swabians The German-speaking minority in the Banat (as distinct from the "Saxons", the German-speaking minority of Transylvania, also in Romania).

Wallachian A term of abuse for Romanians used by German and Magyar speakers in Romania. From the Romanian province of Wallachia.